D1557662

COVENANT

OF A

COLONY

THE POPHAM STORY

BY W. M. BRYAN

Copyright © 2020 William M. Bryan

All rights reserved

The characters and events portrayed in this book are based upon historical fact, however it is written as a story and embellished as such.   No part of this book may be reproduced, or stored in a retrieval system, or transmitted in any form or by any means, electronic, mechanical, photocopying, recording, or otherwise, without express written permission of the publisher.

ISBN-13: 9798635771167

ISBN-10: 1477123456

Cover design by: William M. Bryan

Library of Congress Control Number: 2018675309

Printed in the United States of America

ACKNOWLEDGEMENTS

I would like to thank my wife, Susan L Bryan.
Without her encouragement and support, this novel could not have been written.
A special thanks goes to my editor, Jenny Monteiro

CONTENTS

CHAPTER ONE

The Commission

James Davis walked into the ballroom with a feeling of awe and amazement. It had been years since he had attended an affair at the estate of his family friend, Sir John Popham, Chief Justice of England. It was as large and foreboding as he remembered it and looking around, he could see the families of prominent dignitaries, knights, merchants, spokesmen, naval commanders, and explorers. They were sitting around tables, eating, drinking, visiting and talking with one another while listening to a soft consort of viols, flutes, and lutes. Sir John, as with most of the wealthy in England, invested primarily in real estate. As a result, their estates were opulent and were indicators of how successful they and their families were.

The Davis Family was well respected in Devon. One

with a reputation of very capable seamen, ship masters and captains, yet James was nervous and apprehensive about how he would be received by these men and women of extreme wealth. His older brother, Robert, approached him with a large smile on his bearded face. As a child, it was that smile that would always put James at ease when he was nervous or upset.

"There you are, Boy!" Robert said as he placed his arm around James' shoulder. "Come with me. I have a seat waiting for you."

James, who was 27 years old, always admired his oldest brother Robert, who served his apprenticeship as a young sailor under the great explorer of the new world, Sir Walter Raleigh. At the table, sat his father and mother, Sir Thomas and Lady Elizabeth Davis, and his brother John, and his wife Mary. After affectionately greeting his family, James and Robert joined the table awaiting the beginning of the celebration.

After a few minutes of small talk, the awaited

moment came. Sir John Popham walked to the center of the ballroom and greeted those present. While he was speaking, Sir Ferdinando Gorges, the military governor of Plymouth, joined him. Everyone in the room stood in honor of Sir Ferdinando's position. After a brief pause, he motioned for them all to sit.

"It is with great joy that I share this evening with you all! Tonight we celebrate the start of a new financial venture for you and for England. Last year on April 10, 1606, our gracious and eloquent leader, King James, affixed his signature to a charter for two colonies in America, thus the Virginia Company of Plymouth and the Virginia Company of London were established. As a result, we've spoken to each of you about the benefits of getting financially involved and here we are today. My good friend, Sir Ferdinando Gorges and I have taken particular interest in the Northern Colony - The Plymouth Charter." The crowd applauded.

Sir Ferdinando took the stage to address the crowd. "Many of you know that last August, The Plymouth

Company sent two vessels to explore the coast for the best place to establish our settlement. First we sent the ship *Richard,* under the command of Captain Henry Challons. Then, we sent another vessel under the command of Sir Popham's grandson, Captain Thomas Hanham and Martin Pring. The two were to join forces in the new world but never met. Much to our dismay, we discovered the *Richard* traveled too far south and was captured by the Spanish fleet near Florida."

He paused for a moment. At this point the crowd became loud, displaying anger at the Spaniards, for this had been a far too common occurrence.

"But in spite of not locating the *Robert*, Captain Hanham's vessel was successful in its exploration and came home with the best location for our new settlement," Sir Ferdinando concluded. "At the mouth of the river Sagadahoc."

Sir John continued. "We are thankful for your financial commitment. From all reports, we believe this region has resources and wealth that are unimaginable. Your investments will produce tremendous increase you can be sure!"

The crowd stood and cheered. James looked over the crowd. The excitement he felt was almost uncontrollable to himself and to those around him, but also to his family. His father was the treasurer of the Charter and had always had a keen knowledge of investing.

James spotted a young woman at an adjoining table he had never seen. Having been raised in Devon, he was certain he knew most of the families wealthy enough to participate in such an investment as the Virginia Company. This redheaded beauty however was unfamiliar. He was a bit embarrassed when he realized that he had been staring at her when she turned and gave him a smile.

"Robert, do you know who that young lady is?" James asked.

"I believe she is the daughter of Sir Thomas Keyes of Gloucester. Quite a beauty, isn't she?" Robert could see his brother was interested. "I will ask Father for sure and introduce you to her after our gala."

Everyone sat down and Sir John Popham continued his address to the crowd.

"Since the return of the expedition, we have been working to assemble a group of 120 settlers of many different professions, worthy of the journey. We have soldiers, traders, farmers, craftsmen and carpenters. In just one month from today, in May, two ships will depart on their voyage to establish what we have determined to be called *The Popham Colony*. I would like to read the names of those who have been appointed as leaders of the expedition. As I do, will you please stand and be acknowledged?"

"George Popham, my beloved nephew, has been appointed President." The crowd applauds while George stands.

"Raleigh Gilbert has been appointed Admiral and Second in Command."

"Captain Robert Davis will be the Captain of the

Mary and John. His brother James will be the Master of the Ship, the *Gift of God,* and the Commander of the new fort, *Fort St. George.*"

"Captain John Elliott will be the Captain of the *Gift of God.*"

"And lastly, Chaplain Richard Seymour, will be the expedition's Preacher and also Assistant to the President."

After the crowd was done clapping for the individuals listed, Sir John invited Chaplain Seymour to pray and commit the new colony to the Lord as a work of God. After which, he urged the crowd to continue to fellowship and personally congratulate these leaders.

Immediately, a flood of well wishers arrived at James' table. Before long, Robert appeared with a lovely young lady holding on to his arm.

"James, I would like to introduce you to Rachel. Rachel is the daughter of one of our chief financiers, Sir Thomas Keyes."

Rachel was strikingly beautiful with her long red hair,

warm smile, and gorgeous evening gown. James was at a loss for words. He had never found himself in such a situation before. "Why am I so nervous?" he thought to himself. He paused for a moment with his mouth wide open, unable to speak.

His brother whispered in his ear, "Close your mouth. You look like a cow at a new gate."

"My pleasure to meet you, Rachel. My name is James...Oh wait, you already know that."

Rachel covered her mouth to hide her amusement. "Good evening, James. It is a pleasure meeting you. My father has told me about your family and I'm glad to have finally met you."

There was an obvious connection between James and Rachel. One that compelled James to step out of his comfort zone and ask Rachel after a short pause, "Would you like see the garden? I could escort you and show you the property."

"I would love to." She responded.

Rachel took hold of James' arm and the two went

walking through the doors into the courtyard. As they walked, Robert caught the eye of his younger brother, John, and raised his eyebrow over this odd turn of events.

Springtime at Wellington House in Somerset, England was beautiful. The gardens were immaculately maintained with hedge walkways and seating at every bend. The Bluebells, roses, and Roman Candles were in full bloom producing a captivating fragrance.

As James and Rachel walked the garden, Rachel smiled as she shared, "Gardening is one of my favorite hobbies."

"Oh really?" After a short pause, James asked, "What kind of plant is that?" James pointed to a large, thorny plant surrounded by a circle of small hedges.

"That is the Glastonbury Hawthorn: one of my favorites. There is a lot of mysticism around that plant. According to Celtic tradition, it is the most likely plant to be inhabited by fairies." She smiled.

James was enthralled, "Fairies, huh?"

"Yes. During May Day festivities, we use its flowers to make garlands and decorate yards with the tradition that the flowers will protect the household from evil spirits. But the Glastonbury Hawthorn also has some powerful Christian legends attached to it as well. One legend is that the tree was the source of Jesus' crown of thorns. Another legend is that the staff of Joseph of Arimathea, the man who had Christ's body buried after the crucifixion, was planted here and the Glastonbury Hawthorn grew out of it. Whether any of those legends are true, I don't know, but stories, legends, and tales make our imaginations soar, our lives fun and interesting."

James was captivated, not only by Rachel's beauty on the outside, but by the tenderness and love for life she was beginning to display on the inside.

"Another one of my hobbies is that I like to write and tell stories to the small children in our village. When I have time, I bake tarts, gather the children together and tell them whimsical stories of fairies, animals, and the love of the family. Family is very important to me. Father says your family is a strong family known for its adventurous spirit. Is that true?"

James thought for a moment and smiled. "Yes, I suppose it is. I'm the third Davis son in my family. You've met my older brothers, Richard and John, who are both ship captains as well. My uncle John died just two years ago, but he made a name for himself as an explorer. When he came home from his expeditions, he would sit us boys down and tell us some remarkable stories of the East Indies, the South Atlantic, and his continued search for the Northwest Passage. But I guess, when your closest childhood friends are Sir Walter Raleigh and Sir Humphrey Gilbert, what chance do you have?"

"Wait. Are you telling me your uncle was the legendary John Davis?" Rachel asked. James nodded.

"As far back as I can remember, I've wanted to follow in their footsteps and become a sailor myself. All the stories of distant lands to which they traveled and the different cultures they experienced were captivating."

"Our father isn't a sailor like his brother was, but courageous nonetheless, nurturing that adventurous spirit in us. He has been fearless with his money and entrepreneurial abilities to where our family lives in one of the nicest estates in Devon. Actually, because of his enterprising spirit, he is the treasurer of the Plymouth Company."

"What is life like on board a ship?" Rachel asked.

"Becoming a sailor is not without its labor. To become a sailor, a boy starts as an apprentice when he is about 12 years old. If your father has the means, he pays a hefty sum for a ship's master or a first mate to teach them everything about sailing. After the apprenticeship is over, they too would become a ship's master or first mate."

"A sailor's work includes repairing masts, sails, and hulls from previous voyages, loading supplies, and even hunt game upon reaching land to supplement the food supply."

"Sounds like exhausting work! What has kept you motivated?"

"The goal of knowing you may sometimes be the first

set of English eyes to see a waterfall, mountain, or beach in another land. To set foot and claim a new island or territory for the Crown is a goal. Also, to be recognized as the explorer who discovered a new land for future colonization, which is what we are going to be doing with the Popham Colony or our sister colony, Jamestown."

Rachel was intrigued. "You are on a boat for months at a time. I enjoy the outdoors so much I think my mind would, would, would…explode. What do you do for entertainment?"

"The sailors who travel with you become your family. As their leader, I have to work hard to keep them from fighting each other. They have to stay focused on their jobs. One mistake can cost them, and the rest of us, our lives. When we encounter calm, I give them permission to pull out the fiddle, fife, and tin whistle to play music, sing, and even dance!" He paused and looked into her eyes. "You were talking about Fairies and legends. I think sailors are the most superstitious lot on the planet. We are also, very religious.

Sometimes, the two get mixed together."

"What do you mean by *mixed* together?" Rachel asked.

James explained, "Sailors acknowledge they are in the hands of Almighty God. He protects them from dangers and misfortunes, so they always worship Him while at sea. As the ship's captain, it is expected that I denounce any possibility of offending God. No Swearing, no filthy stories, or blaspheming God in any way is allowed! I cannot allow gambling with dice or cards. Every morning and evening, we will have prayer meetings and read from the Bible. I can be sure you were not aware of it because of superstition, a ship may not begin its voyage on a Friday, because that is the day Christ Jesus was crucified. It could mean a curse on the voyage."

"So what about you, Captain James. Are YOU superstitious?" Rachel asked with a smile.

"Well, let's just say, rather than being superstitious or foolish, I always emphasize that my men keep their focus upon Almighty God as the one who protects them, guides them, and if we as a crew believe that, our mission will always succeed," James responded.

"The scriptures say, *The foolishness of a man twists his way, and his heart frets against the Lord.* When you are at sea, you have to know and believe that everything you are doing is correct. Sometimes, decisions need to be made so quickly that if you give in to foolish thinking, the mission doesn't succeed. "

Rachel was impressed at James' dedication to God. She was reminded of her own parish and how she always felt God's presence when she worshipped there. She had always been an admirer of those who had their faith in the center of their lives. To her, they appeared to be stronger both physically and emotionally. To see that quality in a man was actually something causing her to take an interest in James.

Robert came in from the side of the garden entrance and saw them sitting on the garden bench. With a sigh of relief he said, "There you are James! You're a hard man to find." Then, turning to Rachel, he said, "I'm sorry Miss, my brother is needed inside."

James smiled at Rachel, kissed her hand, and looked into her eyes. "I have truly enjoyed meeting you Rachel. You shared at the beginning of our chat that one of your interests is to write. I also have an interest in that area. Would you mind if I called upon you again? I'd like to hear more."

Smiling, she responded, "The pleasure would be all mine, James. I look forward to seeing you again."

Robert put his arm around his brother's neck and steered him toward the manor. He whispered in his ear as they walked. "Wow little brother, I've never seen that kind of emotion come out of you before. She is beautiful, mind you. I can see why you are interested. But this is so out of character for you." Once again, the smile James adored appeared on his brother's bearded face.

There were six brothers in the Davis household. James was number three. He had a reputation in the Davis Family for being the serious one; details, facts, rules, following orders, the military life suited him well and he was loyal to the crown. He was well respected and his decisions militarily as well as in his personal life always proved to be worth positive recognition. He rarely gave time to frivolous activities, even though one would think otherwise, since he was well loved by all. He seemingly displayed a rare control over his emotions, which enabled him to appear as an unchangeable force when he made his mind up. So when Robert saw how obviously enthralled he was with this young redhead, he was surprised. "Is this the James I have always known?" he thought.

Robert was the oldest of the six Davis brothers. Unlike his brother James, Robert was known for being frank, impulsive and speaking what was on his mind. From a small child, the ocean enthralled him. He loved to fish, always keeping an eye out for an incoming vessel.

He made friends quickly and when a ship came to port, he would be there to welcome the seamen by offering his assistance to help them unload their gear, with the hope of hearing about life on board. He was a natural leader, and at just 11 years old, served his apprenticeship under Sir Humphrey on the barke, *Raleigh*, and its expedition to Newfoundland.

When entering the manor, both James and Robert joined the others who earlier stood before the crowd. The Oath and Covenant of the Plymouth Company had been drawn up and set on the table before them. The *Oath* was a sworn affirmation to be true and faithful to one's promises. The *Covenant* was a solemn promise between two parties. Those who signed, committed to be true and faithful servants to the king: keeping secret all matters concerning same; being circumspect, and agreeable to His Majesty's letters, patents, and directions.

Each took their turn with the quill pen, affixing their signatures to the document: first George Popham, followed by Raleigh Gilbert, James Davis, Robert Davis, Edward Harlie, Ellis Best, Master Gome Carew, and finishing with Rev. Richard Seymour.

The start of a new era of English history and prospect of increased wealth beyond measure was beginning. Everyone present experienced the excitement of the moment.

CHAPTER TWO

Relationships Are Formed

Rachel and the Keyes Family resided a mere eight miles from James' estate in Devon. Their home was just outside of Dunsford; a sweet little village, nestled on the northern edge of Dartmoor. Its thatch, cob, and moorstone cottages are a lovely contrast to the stark countryside full of wild daffodils leading down the valley to the River Teign.

James and Rachel became very close during the month following the event in which they met. He was well received by the Keyes family and a courtship began. James was on his journey to Dunsford, traveling through the preserve on his horse, Abbot, a tall Irish Hobby mare, when he heard a loud voice calling from a wooden thicket.

"Captain Davis! James Davis!" the voice shouted.

James stopped in his tracks and as he searched the

thicket for who spoke his name. He saw two young men coming up the pathway.

He recognized one of the men. "Hey, aren't you that preacher, Seymour? Didn't I meet you at Sir John Popham's estate last month?" Richard Seymour nodded. "What are you doing out here?"

Richard responded with a smile, "We're hunting!" With that, he uncovered a large, canvas bag full of rabbits to show James and held up an archer's bow. "No firearms here."

James remembered the conversation between him and his brother Robert after they were introduced to the preacher the night of the signing of the Oath and Covenant. James asked his brother why they entrusted such a big responsibility upon someone was so young as the preacher. His brother told him "Don't be deceived, brother, he may look like a young peasant, but I've been told he is a brilliant Oxford graduate, and a personal friend of the Bishop."

James looked at the smiling faces of the two men.

Richard was obviously proud of the fact that he had been using a bow and arrow to hunt the rabbits. Since the advent of the musket, archery was increasingly becoming a sport of the elite. The man next to Richard appeared to be a foreigner.

"Awe, yes!" James said. " It's good to know there are still archers practicing their skill...such a rarity in this modern age of muskets. You snagged all of those rabbits yourself, did you? That's not an easy feat. How did you get to be so good?"

"I've been practicing. Have you ever met my companion, Skidwarres? He's been schooling me in the use of a bow and arrow." Skidwarres tipped his hat in acknowledgement of Captain James.

"Skidwarres? You must be the Pemaquid native I've heard so much about. I was hoping to meet you at some time, but I sure didn't think it would be in the forest, during a hunting expedition." James chuckled as he dismounted his horse and reached out his hand to shake Skidwarres' hand.

James remembered hearing of the excitement of the

mariners in the Plymouth community when, at the conclusion of a previous exploration of the new continent, Captain George Weymouth introduced five young Pemaquid natives he brought back with him to England: Dehanada, a sagamo or commander, Amaret, Skidwarres, Maneddo, and a native servant called Assacomoit.

Captain Weymouth turned the natives over to Sir Ferdinand Gorges to teach them English and hopefully get information about the coastline and the best places for planting the colony.

After learning English, two of the natives, Assacomoit and Maneddo, were used as interpreters on the *Richard,* which was the ship lost to the Spaniards. The sagamo, Dehanada, had been the interpreter for the vessel commanded by Captains Hanham and Pring. He was left there, so only the two natives, Amaret and Skidwarres were still being tutored in England.

"Very nice meet you, Captain James," said Skidwarres in broken English. "Richard have good eye.

Good marksman!" He paused. "What about you, Captain? Can you shoot arrow?"

Skidwarres handed him the bow assuming James would make a feeble attempt to use it as most other Englishmen he had met. What he didn't know was that James was the number one archer in his class at university.

He jokingly picked up the bow acting as if he didn't know what he was doing, grabbed an arrow and said, "Any rabbits close by?"

Skidwarres and Richard looked at each other with a humorous smile. Then James said, "No rabbits? OK...how about that mouse over there on the tree?" The tree was 30 yards away and the thought of being able to hit a moving mouse on it was hilarious.

Before anyone could comment, James focused on the target, released the arrow and pinned the varmint to the tree! Needless to say, Captain James' respect level instantly grew.

"So, how did you two end up together?" James asked.

"Sir Ferdinand Gorges asked if I would tutor Skidwarres here in the English language and culture. He and I are both the same age and because of my connection to the church, he was also leaning on me to convert him. I'm happy to say he was baptized this last March! Actually, the tutoring has been double-sided. I love to learn and I'm learning as much about the Pemaquid culture as he is the English." Richard continued, "I'm so looking forward to our upcoming expedition, to see for myself what the Pemaquid seacoast looks like. I'm hoping to convince Chief Justice Popham to allow Skidwarres to travel with us as our interpreter."

"I'll put in a good word for him, Preacher. Well, as much as I would enjoy spending more time with you both," James said while mounting his horse, "I have someone waiting for me. Nice meeting you, Skidwarres."

James rode off down the path toward Dunsford, the morning sun warming him. Upon passing through the gate of the Keyes estate, he noticed Rachel at the porch near the entrance to the garden.

She was arranging some newly-cut lavender flowers in a ceramic vase, her loyal Foxhound, Bonny, was at her feet. Bonny noticed James first, jumped to her feet and darted out across the yard to greet him. The reception was great.

"Down girl!" James joyfully exclaimed as he petted Bonny's head, "Want to take me to your mistress?" Together, they walked toward the garden where Rachel was finishing her arrangement.

"I've never seen anything so beautiful," exclaimed James.

"Yes, they are! I'm trying to capture the last of the late-bloomers from my garden." Rachel said while placing the last Lavender flower in the vase.

James laughed, "I wasn't talking about the flowers...!"

Rachel blushed as she realized he was flirting with her. She turned around and ran over to him, giving him a warm embrace. "James, I can't imagine what it will be like not seeing you for months. I'm going to miss you so much.

What if something happens to you? The *Richard* was captured by the Spanish and we have no idea what happened to its crew. I don't want to live without you in my life!"

James was surprised at Rachel's declaration of love for him. His heart warmed because he felt the same way regarding her. He placed his hands on both side of her face and looked her in the eyes, "I don't want to live my life without you either."

The two kissed for the first time.

"Don't be afraid of me not returning. The reason the *Richard* didn't return was because it wasn't captained by the famous Captains James and Robert Davis." He sarcastically smiled.

"Remember what the book of Proverbs says? 'In the mouth of a fool is a rod of pride, but the lips of the wise will preserve them.' So, which are you James, proud or wise?" Rachel teased him.

"You see? How can anything possibly happen to our expedition when someone so spiritual is praying for me to make it home safely?"

James realized that the voyage would of course have its moments of concern no matter how much planning is done. A Captain and a Master of a ship both have to make tough calls and speedy decisions and there are many obstacles to overcome at sea: weather, wind, pirates, disease, & navigation - let alone trying to keep the crew from killing each other. Much has to do with respect and trust of leadership. But at the end, one thing wins out…adventure!

At this point, the Keyes family steward came to the door. "Lunch has been prepared in the dining room, my Lady." He held the door for both Captain James and Rachel to enter.

They dined and spent the rest of the afternoon sharing stories of their childhood and what they enjoyed most as children. They didn't want their visit to come to an end but as the sun began to set, James realized he needed time to ride back to Davis Manor.

He began to think about all of the things that had to

come together before the departure of the expedition.

Rachel walked James outside to the porch. Rachel boldly asked, "A kiss for good luck?"

"Of course!" James responded. They kissed.

"Wait right here James. I have something I think you'll like." Rachel ran into the house.

While he was waiting for her, he reached down and petted Bonny. "I'm going to miss you girl. Protect your mistress while I'm gone."

Rachel entered the porch carrying a canvas sack. "I made something for you James. It's a way you will remember me every day of your time spent on your journey." She reached inside the bag and pulled out a beautiful, handmade book with parchment pages and a leather cover. It was strapped together with the finest twine Rachel could find. "It's a journal. Since I can't go with you, I thought you could write a summary of each day of your journey and when we see each other again, you can share your trip with me. I don't want to miss one detail!"

"God bless you Rachel. This is absolutely beautiful. I vow to you that every time I open this journal to write in, I will think of you and say a prayer for you." James was amazed at the skills and abilities Rachel had.

"Every book has a title." Rachel commented, " The first page is a page designed just for that purpose."

James opened to the first page where Rachel had drawn a boarder of flowers from her garden. In the middle was an empty rectangle.

"What are you going to name yours, James?" Rachel asked.

James thought for a moment, "I think I will title it, *A Relation of a Voyage to Sagadahoc.*" James placed it back in its sack, mounted Abbot and rode off through the gate toward home.

CHAPTER THREE

The Expedition Begins

May 30, 1607 was a sunny, late spring day on the Southern English Coast. The two ships, *"The Gift of God"* and the *"Mary and John"* were docked at Sutton's Pool, the harbor of Plymouth. The crews of the two ships were busy loading supplies on board. So much activity precedes a voyage of this magnitude.

Captain James and his brother Robert arrived in their carriage, unloaded their chests and were welcomed by the Master's Servant, Anthony. Anthony enthusiastically handed a list to each Captain. "Good day, Captain James! Good day, Captain Robert! These on the list are who you'll expect to join you today, Sirs."

The *Mary and John*, a 400-ton ship, was to be commanded by Sir Raleigh Gilbert and captained by Robert

Davis. Robert was to confirm that each participant on his list was accounted for.

The *"Gift of God,"* a 200-ton, flat-bottomed Flyboat, was to be commanded by Sir George Popham. It would be captained by John Elliot and Captain James would be its Navigator. He was to also confirm that each participant on his list was accounted for.

The Master's Servant Anthony's primary duty at this point was to make sure there was enough food and water being loaded for the two ships as well as the other necessary supplies: candles, firewood, brooms, buckets, and the sailor's sea chests.

In addition to the ship's officers and the seamen, the *Mary and John* would carry eighty colony planters consisting of soldiers, a few farmers, a blacksmith, an experienced shipwright, and some "riff-raff" or common laborers. The *Gift of God* would carry an additional forty planters, consisting also of a few farmers, carpenters, a cooper or barrel-maker, a geologist to search for profitable metals, and

Seymour the preacher.

James looked around at the docks, the people filling them, and the beautiful Plymouth harbor with the towering walls of Plymouth Castle to the west. Before a voyage, he enjoyed standing still on the dock, taking in the sights, praying under his breath, remembering his family and the remarkable childhood experiences he had here in Devon.

Some said he was privileged and that he admitted was true. He was privileged to have a father and mother who supported his desires to become a ship captain. There were plenty of other opportunities to advance in society and make a name for yourself when your family was as influential as the Davis family. Yet his father Thomas, believed in letting his children follow after their hearts. He didn't have to be coerced into supporting James when he followed in his older brothers' footsteps and was selected to do his apprenticeship as a young lad.

"God has called me to be an investor. A successful one at that," James remembered his father saying, " But you, my boys…God has given you all an adventurous spirit! He has called you to do remarkable things, explore new worlds, and be leaders of others!"

Adventurous spirit? Sometimes James wondered if it was being adventurous or just stupid. He thought back to when he was just 12 years old and serving his apprenticeship. He found himself in a storm and he and another apprentice were the ones who had to furl, or roll up the sail, securing it to the yard to compensate for the wind. With rain pouring down and gale-force winds, they took off their shoes as routine safety, so they wouldn't slip while climbing the ropes. James had a rush of excitement mixed with fear as he was going to finally test what he had been training for.

Making their way to about 50 feet above the deck, fingers numb from the cold, they were hit by an unexpected gust of wind. Both were swept off the yard and began to fall when James instinctively grabbed a rigging that had snapped; saving his life. The other young lad wasn't so fortunate. He was swept out to sea and never seen again.

It didn't matter who you were at that point; privileged or common *"riff-raff."* Most who fell from the yard in similar situations, fell to their death onto the deck or into the waves, the chances of being rescued was extremely slim. Experiences such as that formed a man out of a boy; one who could think quickly, respect life, and respect the sea.

James and Robert went their separate ways taking their chests to their cabins aboard their vessels. James acknowledged sailors as he passed, who were preparing the *Gift of God* for its voyage, by sewing its sails, scraping, re-caulking and tarring its hull. By the time he made it back down to the dock, a line of colony planters had begun to form.

Captain James pulled out his list and began to confirm those traveling on his ship.

At this point, the preacher, Richard Seymour, along with Skidwarres, approached Captain James with their two small chests.

"We have an addendum to the list you are holding,

Captain." Richard handed him a document sealed with the seal of President George Popham. "Skidwarres will be joining our expedition as our translator and guide. After much prayer and negotiation, Sir Popham was open to the idea. After all, who would be better to lead us in an unknown land than one who was born and raised there?"

James smiled in approval. "I see on the list that you, Richard, are not only our chaplain but also Sir Popham's personal secretary. I'm sure that helped him to make this decision. He is fortunate to have secured such a brilliant young man and such a great marksman!" he chuckled, "You'll make sure no rabbits are stowing aboard, right, Richard?" They joined in a friendly laugh together.

"Commander Popham has requested you to bunk in his quarters, and Skidwarres will be just outside. We'll see you in the morning for our departure blessing." James paused and focused on the native. "Welcome Skidwarres. I look forward to getting to know you better on our voyage."

Richard and the native, Skidwarres, disappeared up

the plank onto the *Gift of God*.

The day was drawing to a close as Captain James continued to meet and greet those on his list. When everyone was accounted for, he went up to his quarters to prepare for a night of sleep before the early morning departure. As he unloaded his chest, he removed the journal given to him by Rachel and placed it on his desk. His heart warmed as he thought of his new love. He said a quick prayer.

"Lord Almighty, I thank you for bringing Rachel into my life. You've placed a desire in my heart for her that is incomparable to any other, but I know you also have placed me here, to be a part of this expedition. So, what I'm saying Lord, is I trust you will protect her in my absence and bring me safely home. Lord, I am in your hands. " With that being said, James curled his pillow under his head and fell fast asleep.

Commander George Popham and his secretary, Richard were in the large cabin at the stern of the *Gift of God*, while Captain Elliott and Captain Davis had smaller, windowless cabins but also in the stern. The crew and planters slept on hammocks beneath the deck.

Chief Justice John Popham and Sir Ferdinando Gorges had strategically selected the leaders of the expedition. The accomplishments and reputation of each leader was well known by them.

Sir John Popham, had been Chief Justice of England since 1592, was well-known in all circles and had tremendous influence. As a privileged youngster, his reputation was legendary as one of drinking, gambling, affiliation with negative riff-raff and in his boredom, sought high-risk activities and was even suspected to be an occasional Highwayman, or robber. As he matured, the loss of his father affected him tremendously along with the inherited responsibility of his position, landholdings, and wealth. He settled down enough to marry and take up the other side of the law. He studied law and became a judge. Because of his insight into both the lifestyle of the lawful and that of the lawless, he gained a feared reputation for calling it as it was, achieving the nick-name, "The Hanging Judge."

Sir Ferdinando Gorges on the other hand had extensive military training on land and sea as a young man. He made his trusted reputation while serving as a captain in France. He was captured and imprisoned in Spain in 1588 and wounded in Paris in 1589. He was knighted in 1591 and sent to Plymouth to command the fortifications there. While there, he discovered he and the Chief Justice were actually related by marriage. They became close allies as a result and when the opportunity to finance and organize the Plymouth Charter came, there wasn't anyone who could have done it better than they.

Sir John Popham's nephew, George, had been the Customer of Bridgewater Port in Somerset. He was the chief Customs officer who collected all the customs dues and recorded all of the entries and exits into the port. His reputation was not one of being a hero on the battlefield, but one of being extremely organized, loyal to the crown, and able to see things completed efficiently and purposefully. He had been enchanted however by the stories he heard of distant lands and discoveries from the ships entering Somerset. He wasn't the classic individual to head up the start of a colony. He was a tall, portly fellow who was already in his late fifties, out of shape, and suffering from obvious bouts of arthritis as the weather turned cold. However, when he heard about the charter and the prospect of claiming the Sagadahoc area for the crown, he approached his uncle for the opportunity to experience the excitement. His uncle agreed. He knew if anyone would see the new Fort St. George constructed, it would be his nephew.

Sir Raleigh Gilbert, Commander of the *Mary and John,* had a stellar reputation as a ship captain and had grown up in a home full of navigators and explorers. His father was Sir Humphrey Gilbert, who was also the half-brother of Sir Walter Raleigh; hence his son's name-Raleigh Gilbert. The Gilberts and Davis' had been childhood neighbors, therefore Sir Raleigh had a long time friendship with the Davis Family. He served his apprenticeship alongside of Robert Davis under his father Humphrey. He was confident that with Robert as his ship's captain, they were going to see success.

At last, the greatly anticipated morning came. The skies were clear and the sun would soon be rising up over the wall of Fort Plymouth. The crew gathered for a quick breakfast of pork and oatmeal and then soon assembled on the dock between the two ships and some listening over the rails of the ships themselves.

Richard Seymour, the preacher, arrived and moved to the center of the crowd carrying his Book of Common Prayer. With a loud voice he addressed them. "Today is a monumental day in our English history. Today, we begin a journey to plant an English settlement, in honor of our beloved King James, in the new world. All of you listening to me have a part to play in this journey. We want to say that _WE_ hand-selected you for this task but truth be told, it's our _God_ who has hand-selected each of you! Your skills and crafts, knowledge, experience, and leadership qualities will be put to use on this voyage, you can be sure! With that, it is my responsibility to sanctify this voyage for what is to come. Only God knows what we shall encounter, and what we shall humbly accept so with that said, let us begin."

At this point, the men removed their hats to show honor to God. The Preacher opened his book. "The Lord be with thee," Seymour began.

"And also with thee!" shouted the men in traditional liturgical response.

Seymour continued, "Lord we go with you. We are safe with you. We do not travel alone, for your hand is upon us. Your protection is divine. Besides, in front and behind, You encircle our lives, for we are yours and you are ours. Now, listen closely as I read Psalm 23."

"The LORD is my shepherd; I shall not want.

He maketh me to lie down in green pastures: he leadeth me beside the still waters.

He restoreth my soul: he leadeth me in the paths of righteousness for his name's sake.

Yea, though I walk through the valley of the shadow of death, I will fear no evil: for thou art with me; thy rod and thy staff they comfort me.

Thou preparest a table before me in the presence of mine enemies: thou anointest my head with oil; my cup runneth over.

Surely goodness and mercy shall follow me all the days of my life: and I will dwell in the house of the LORD for ever."

Seymour closed his book and motioned for the men to join him in this final recitation of the Lord's Prayer.

"Our Father, which art in heaven, Hallowed be thy Name. Thy kingdom come. Thy will be done in earth, as it is in heaven. Give us this day our daily bread. And forgive us our trespasses, as we forgive them that trespass against us. And lead us not into temptation; But deliver us from evil: For thine is the kingdom, the power, and the glory, For ever and ever. Amen."

With the conclusion of the service, the cannons from Fort Plymouth fired a celebratory salute to the departing explorers and planters. The Master's Servant, Martin, blew his whistle and shouted "All Aboard!" After everyone returned to their ships, the crew hurried to their respective places, released lines and set sail toward The Lizard.

The Lizard Peninsula and the entrance to Falmouth Harbor in Southern Cornwall is the last point of the English coastline to pass before hitting the high seas. It would be approached within the day and so between Plymouth and Falmouth, the crews checked for any leaks in the ship's hull, tears in the sail, or any other problem that might cause the ship to be in danger. If they noticed anything, the common practice was to stop then at Falmouth and make repairs before moving on.

All looked good on both vessels, so it looked as if there would be no stopping at Falmouth Harbor. Captain James was standing on deck with Captain Elliott peering at the coastline when Richard Seymer and Skidwarres joined them. Lizard Lighthouse on Lizard Point was coming clearly into view. The sun was beginning to fall behind its tower.

"I'm not from these parts, and even though I'm an Oxford graduate, I'm having a difficult time explaining to

Skidwarres here why we would call this point, The Lizard."
Seymour commented with a smile. "Perhaps you can help
me?"

Captain Elliott was somewhat of a historian. He loved
British geology and map-making was one of his hobbies. He
addresses the question posed by Seymour. "Actually, the
name Lizard is a corruption of the Cornish name, *Liz Ardh*.
Liz Ardh means *High Court*."

He continued, "Lizard Point Lighthouse is the last
structure seen when sailing away from England and the first
to see upon returning. It was erected by Sir John Killigrew at
his own expense. He saw the need to protect the vessels
traveling by. With the Lizard Reef and the rough coastline,
sailing in and out of the harbor here is quite hazardous
causing this area to be nicknamed *The Graveyard of Ships*.
There is a curious thing however about *The Lizard*. It
actually has a supernatural abundance of common Lizards,
Sand Lizards and the Slow Worm, which is a kind of legless
lizard, abiding among the rocks on the shore."

The day was coming to a close as a beautiful sunset was beginning to appear off on the horizon. As the *Gift of God* and the *Mary and John* traveled past the lighthouse, the light illuminated. What a fitting way to end the day and say goodbye to glorious England!

Once he returned to his cabin, James pulled out his journal and wrote the title on the front page, *Relation of a Voyage to Sagadahoc.* Then he prayed, "Lord protect and guard my sweet Rachel until I return. Protect my brother Robert, my crew here, and those traveling on the *Mary and John* and forgive us of any sins we may have committed."

He opened to the first page, pulled out his quill pen and ink, and began to write his summary of day number one:

"Departed from the Lizard the first day of June, Anno Domini 1607, being Monday about six o'clock in the afternoon. We first traveled northeast, then directed our course for the islands of Flores and Corvo..."

CHAPTER FOUR

Travel Through the Azores

Captain James, his brother Captain Robert, Captain John Elliott, Commander George Popham and Sir Raleigh Gilbert sat at a wooden table in a shaded area on the beach, drinking tankards of ale while taking account of the voyage's successful moments and strategically planning the next portion. The aroma of grilled fish filled the air. After 28 days at sea, what could be better than feasting and resting on such a beautiful beach?

They were headed for the port of Santa Cruz on the island of Flores in the Azores to replenish supplies, but decided to stop at Corvo first. The smaller island was full of waterfalls and picturesque creeks emptying into the Atlantic. It seemed like the perfect place to bathe, swim, play, fish, and stock up with fresh water before the long journey to

America. They discovered it was a treasure trove of fish as well! It wasn't long before the crew had caught more than 200 Grouper, Mackerel and Snapper, prompting them to celebrate with a dynamic fish fry!

The crew had become very close over the past 28 days at sea and the five leaders sitting around the table had grown appreciative of them all. The other passengers, called the "planters," also got to know each of the crew by their first names. They knew who to ask for specific needs they had and visa versa. When the barrel full of ale, accidentally slid out of its holder and split in two, they knew they could go directly to Ralph, the "cooper" or barrel maker. When they needed help with finding anything on board, they knew they could count on the young Seaman Apprentice, Walter. If they were in the mood for music, Alfred, Edgar, and Henry were always anxiously ready to lighten the atmosphere with their fiddle, pennywhistle, and fife.

As they talked, Captain Robert noticed the crowd playing a game in the sand that he was unfamiliar with.

"What sport is it that they are playing? Have any of you ever seen that before? It's most unusual."

Captain James quickly responded. "It's a game known as *Bowl and Dice*. The Permaquids call it *Hubbub*. The native, Skidwarres, taught it to us. He said if we were going to make friends with the natives at all, we needed to learn the game all of his kinsmen play. He said it was not uncommon for one village to challenge another village with the stakes being furs, skins, and other popular treasures. It is easy to learn but does require some skill. He taught it to those of us on the *Gift*. It has been a great pastime and sparks unity for all onboard. I imagine, you'll be saying the same thing real soon."

"While we are on the subject, what is your take on Skidwarres?" asked Sir Raleigh Gilbert. "Do you think he is one we can trust our lives to?"

The three leaders from the *Gift of God* looked at each other and nodded their heads.

"Skidwarres has grown on all of us." James

---

commented, "He has won our trust. The crew has nicknamed him *Skiddy*. He hardly seems like a man who was forcefully taken away from his family. I believe it was a very strategic move by Sir Ferdinand to place him under the tutorage of Richard Seymer. His time with the preacher has turned him. He has learned our language and we know he has converted to Christianity. In observing him, there's very little the bloke can't do well."

The crowd of players shouted loudly, laughing at one another's skills in the game as they ran past the table.

George Popham raised an eyebrow. "He has given us much information about his people and the land he was taken from…enough for us to know what to expect when we arrive. He has agreed to lead us to his people so we can establish relations and begin trading in exchange for his release."

"He doesn't harbor hard feelings against the English?" asked Commander Gilbert.

"The preacher has convinced him of the need for forgiveness," replied Popham.

Gilbert commented, "Forgiveness, huh? If I were in his situation, I don't know if I could ever forgive. I don't know if I agree with Captain Weymouth's idea of taking captives."

"I guess time will tell. That whole idea is a new one to all of us," James replied. "It would have definitely gone different if we would have treated the natives as prisoners, but we didn't. Instead, we treated them well, taught them well, and gave them much freedom. As a result, and I can't speak for the other four natives, but I believe Skiddy has made friends in the process: English friends he is comfortable with and has developed a trust in. Don't mention the Spanish around him though. He has a different view of the Spanish, altogether. When he heard that two of the tribesmen who were brought back with Weymouth, Assacomoit and Maneddo, were captured and killed by the Spaniards, he turned into a savage beast! He looked like a teapot ready to explode! I never saw that side of him before."

James stood up and looked at his brother Robert. "I

need to stretch a bit. Let's go for a stroll, brother." Robert agreed and the two of them took off walking along the shore.

"How's life on the *Mary and John*? Is Commander Gilbert treating you well?" asked James. "He seems like a good fellow, living up to his reputation. But then you know him better than I, since you served your apprenticeship with him. I'm curious. Is it difficult to submit to someone whom you've grown up with and got into mischief with while you were young lads?"

"If anything brother, I would say I respect him more because I know what he is capable of. I know the *real* Raleigh Gilbert and must say I'm proud to serve as his captain. He respects me as well." replied Robert.

"He is definitely a capable commander and seaman! But I must say I'm surprised that he would be willing to leave that life by planting a colony for the Crown. Building a settlement is a lot of hard work! I would think if he wanted to settle down, he would just stay home. Very few ship captains are in line to inherit such a vast estate as that obtained by his father, Sir Humphrey Gilbert, yet Raleigh is moving to start a new life in another country." commented James.

"The other night, over ale, we were sharing thoughts and fears about the trip and he informed me that he wasn't in line to inherit the Gilbert estate. He is the last of six sons in the Gilbert house. When his father Sir Humphrey died, his oldest brother John inherited all of his father's holdings. John is healthy and was just married. When he has a child, the estate will no doubt go to his child. If he were to die childless, the holdings would go to the next brother in line. So, at home, Raleigh will never rise up to the status he wants. At least by being a part of this planting, he will earn a place in history and make a name for himself."

"Oh I see. Now that makes sense." James thought for a moment. "It's been quite a joy traveling with you, brother."

Robert gave him that bearded smile once again. "Now let me ask YOU something, James. How are you fairing without the beautiful Rachel Keyes? Do you think of her often? Do you think you'll ask for her hand anytime soon?"

"Now don't laugh, brother, but when I think of her it's as if my heart beats faster. I didn't tell you Rachel made me a beautiful journal to log an account of our trip in fine detail. She said that way she too can experience the trip as if she were on board with me. So, as often as I can, I say a prayer for her and I write a summary of each day in the journal."

"Oh my! Sounds like I'll be attending a wedding sometime soon. Ha!" At that, Robert put his arm around his brother's neck and punched him playfully in his chest.

The two of them continued to chat as they sat on a log at the side of the creek that emptied into the ocean. They were walking back towards the group when they observed some of the passengers and crew of the *Mary and John* beginning to return to their ship on their longboats. Commander Gilbert was waving at the two men to get their attention.

"I suppose we should hurry up, Robert. There's obviously something transpiring up there."

Commander Gilbert approached Captain Robert. "We've surmised that we need to depart so we can make the port of Santa Cruz. The Master's Servant Martin has taken inventory and we realize we need to load up on supplies again before setting sail to North America. The men are loading now and as soon as we join them, we will be on our course."

"What about the *Gift of God*, Commander?" asked James.

"Popham has decided to let your men enjoy themselves 'til nightfall and depart first thing in the morning to join us in Santa Cruz." Gilbert replied.

With that being said, Robert said goodbye to his brother James and departed with Commander Gilbert to the remaining longboat on the beach. The passengers and crew of the *Gift* watched as the *Mary and John* sailed off in the distance.

Once nightfall hit, the game activities ceased and a couple fires were made so all could celebrate and enjoy the time left on the beach before heading back to the ship. Alfred, Edgar, and Henry with their fiddle, pennywhistle, and fife played whilst some of the others danced a jig.

"The Spaniards are here!" shouted a strong voice from the water. "A longboat is coming!"

The music stopped among gasps of unbelief. Fear gripped the crowd as everyone either scurried at attention or for cover. The English grabbed their muskets and poised themselves for what may be an ambush. The Spanish were not to be trusted. Why were they making themselves so vulnerable by arriving in a longboat? Was it a tactic to get all to focus on the longboat and its passengers while posing an attack from the rear? Night had fallen and it was extremely dark on the water.

Captain James picked up his spyglass and tried to find the ship from where the longboat was launched. He located it and noticed it was not flying a Spanish flag, but a tri-color orange, white and blue flag, which James concluded meant the ship was Dutch and not Spanish.

"At ease! The ship is Dutch, not Spanish!" shouted James.

The Dutch had a reputation for being privateers and could get a bit rowdy but generally had a decent relationship with the English. Captain James cautiously decided to welcome the visitors and treat them with the customary kindness afforded allies of the Crown. As the longboat landed, he greeted the captain of the ship. His name was Captain Hartman.

"I would like to invite you and your men to rest, have a meal, and share some ale with us, Captain." James said. "We caught a tremendous amount of fish today and my cook has prepared an incredible feast as a result."

"We appreciate the hospitality," said Captain Hartman. His men then lined up to be served, after which they sat near the warmth of the fire. The Dutch were on one side and the English facing them on the other. The Dutch were especially kin to the taste of the ale. The more they drank, the more open and loose their conversation became.

"Where are you traveling from, Captain?" James asked.

"We were exploring the land just north of Spanish Florida, when we encountered a Spanish Galleon ready to fight. They didn't know what they were getting into though," the captain bragged, "My men never shy away from a good fight!"

This drew the attention of Captain James and his crew. They drew closer to hear more. The Dutch of course were becoming more intoxicated and freely speaking their minds.

"After an hour of battle and attempts for them to get aboard our ship, they turned sail and forged away thru the sea as quickly as possible." He added, "Those Spanish were cowards!"

By that time the crowd listening to the story was shouting loudly in agreement, "Spanish! Cowards! Spanish! Cowards!"

The captain continued, "When we regrouped, we

recounted our steps and tried to figure out how we could have navigated so far to the south without knowing we were entering into Spanish territory. That's when we realized we had a Spanish spy among us! I have been warned by my admiral that the Spaniards are intent upon conquering all of the land along the coast and the best way to do that is to know the actions of the crew. Almost every Dutch and English ship is vulnerable to harboring a Spanish spy, and it's important to always know those among our crews. Never assume you do not have a spy on board. So, after much thought, we concluded our navigator, Michael, had steered us there on purpose!"

The crowd gasped in unbelief.

"My men went through his chest and found a hand-drawn Spanish map of the very area we were in. Everything was written in Spanish and that sealed our accusations. So, his real name was Miguel, not Michael as we had been told."

One of the men in the crowd asked, "What happened to him?"

"He walked the plank!" He said, "Good riddance to the spy!" With that last statement, the crowd cheered and the captain lifted up his mug as if to toast.

"You're quite the storyteller, Captain Hartman," James humorously responded.

Captain Hartman and his men were pretty well intoxicated by now. The more they drank, the more testy they became of the crew of the *Gift of God* and their purpose for sailing to north America. The Dutch sailing crews were known to often challenge others and become competitive.

All of the talk of the Spaniards was particularly intriguing to Skidwarres. As Captain James had commented, he held a strong grudge with them over the demise of his native friends. Skidwarres drew closer to the fire to hear more when one of the Dutch officers noticed him.

"Redskin!" he shouted and spit out a mouthful of drink while he pointed at Skidwarres to alert all those present.

There wasn't a question as to why he would be upset

upon seeing a Native American in this crowd of English. After all, the Dutch, as well as the Spanish, French, and Portuguese had heard horrific stories of encounters with natives in the New World, whether it was North America, South America, or the Caribbean. For the most part, the natives were not pleased by the European exploration and conquest of their homeland and reacted sometimes violently in return. This produced a fear among most seamen.

As quickly as that was shouted, the Dutch crew responded by grabbing Skidwarres as if he were a threat. They pulled him away from the fire, instinctively pulling out their knives.

The English in turn pulled their mate Skidwarres free and a huge ruckus began: punches being thrown, threats being shouted, man against man. Suddenly, Captain James fired a shot from his musket into the air to get their attention. After a moment, the silence was broken.

"Why would you house a redskin?" shouted Captain Hartman. "They are no good! A danger to us all!"

"You will leave him alone! He is a member of my crew!" replied Captain James

"A member of your crew? (pause) A member of your crew? Have you lost your mind? Hartman asked Captain James. "You might as well ask a viper to be on your crew! "

By this time, the crew had pushed Skidwarres behind them, holding him still, so he could not react to the comments. The English had obviously won the skirmish and displayed the upper hand.

An ally before had never challenged James like this. His training in etiquette came to mind as he remembered his oath for the King and the Plymouth Charter. As much as he didn't wish to police those whom he represented, Captain James composed himself and looking eye to eye with Captain Hartman said, "It is time for you and your crew to return to your ship, Captain. I would suggest you depart in haste."

After a minute of staring face to face between the two captains, the Dutch crew boarded their longboats and rowed to their vessel.

James was happy that the incident ended without anyone getting killed. He looked at his crew and passengers as they were enthusiastically hugging and shaking hands with their native friend Skiddy.

He turned to Commander Popham and commented, "I believe this answers any questions we may have had as to whether Skiddy is accepted by his mates. Wouldn't you agree, Commander?" They smiled.

Once on board the *Gift of God*, Captain James settled in his cabin, got on his knees and thanked the Lord for a great outcome of what could have been a disastrous day. Then as was his custom, he prayed for Rachel and opened his journal to log today's experiences.

CHAPTER FIVE

Land Ho!

The *Gift* departed early in the morning from the Island of Corvo to rendezvous with the *Mary and John* in Santa Cruz on the Island of Flores. It was the 29th of June. As Captain James looked back at the beach where they had spent the entire day before, he couldn't help but appreciate the hand of God and the wonders of His creation. "How much beauty can one place contain?" he thought to himself. The weather and wind was perfect, the morning sun, bouncing its beams off the still waters and then, there were breathtaking waterfalls in the background! He breathed in the fresh ocean air and allowed his senses to take it all in for as long as he could before focusing in on the tasks ahead of him. This morning could have ended up much different had the skirmish gotten out of hand last night. He couldn't help but wonder what it would have done to his reputation as an English leader.

The men had played and drank more than usual while on the beach. As a result, the morning found them a bit groggy and slow to react. As he was making his rounds, James came upon Skidwarres who was quietly sharpening the blade of his knife while sitting on the upper deck. He sat down next to him and putting his hand on Skidwarres' shoulder, James said, "I'm thankful to God that things turned out the way they did last night, Skiddy. You are safe this morning."

Skidwarres looked down at his knife while speaking in his broken English. "Me almost forgot how different I am. I spend much time with English. Skidwarres forget, me not English too."

James thought for a moment, "And it should be obvious to you that even though you have no native family with you, the crew thinks of you as part of their family. They are even willing to lay down their lives for your safety."

Skidwarres broke a smile. "Skidwarres show you his family. You meet them soon!"

"Yes, Skiddy. Yes, I will indeed," James replied. He continued his rounds.

Their ship arrived at Santa Cruz in the late afternoon. They spotted the *Mary and John* docked at the port and anchored alongside of it. The crew was busy loading supplies, food, and fresh water. James spotted his brother Robert on the dock commanding and giving orders to his crew. The crew of the *Gift of God* joined in the process of unloading their barrels and crates and refilling them with food and water as well.

"There's something I need to tell you little Brother," Robert shouted as James approached him. "Since the beginning of the voyage, I have been frustrated that I was assigned such an inexperienced Ship's Master. To say we have locked horns a few times is definitely an understatement. I don't agree with much of his tactics and he obviously doesn't respect me the way he should. The *Mary and John* is the largest ship of its kind in his Majesty's Royal fleet and therefore needs someone to navigate who has a reputation for such. Navigating around the upcoming islands and inlets of the New World is no easy chore."

Robert paused for a moment and looked at James for an upcoming response. "I have requested a change in my crew. I want you, James, to be our Ship's Master for the remainder of our voyage. If approved, Master Anthony will assume your role on the *Gift*. After Gilbert and Popham discuss the matter, I should hear soon."

The thought of working with his brother Robert was welcoming. He had built a bond with the crew of the *Gift* but it was indeed a smaller, faster craft that could be easily handled by someone with less experience. When he was first given the assignment, he also wondered why, with his abilities, he was to be on the *Gift* rather than the *Mary and John*. He soon remembered the "unwritten, and somewhat superstitious rule" that two family members shouldn't serve on the same vessel.

Robert looked over James' shoulder and saw Captain Gilbert on the deck of the *Gift* giving him the hand signal of approval. "Deal is done, Little Brother. We are a team." That being said, Robert gave James his customary bearded smile along with an arm around his neck and playful punch to his chest. "Let's get your gear."

James met with Master Anthony and confirmed that he knew the course westward given to them by previous expeditions to America, and a proposed island harbor where the two ships would meet should they lose sight of each other on the open sea.

They prepared to depart the next morning, being the first day of July 1607 from Santa Cruz. The weather and wind was perfect to engage in the journey. The *Gift of God* departed first, caught the wind, and quickly moved to the edge of the bay, headed toward the open sea.

The *Mary and John* was prepared to depart as well when Captain Robert was told that two of their passengers were unaccounted for. Rumor was that they were being held in the jail for disorderly conduct the previous night. This typically meant that the island police wanted to extract a payoff one last time. Commander Gilbert would need to go and negotiate their return, which could take about an hour or more. Realizing this delay, James signaled the *Gift of God* to slow down by hoisting the *Mary and John's* sail up and down 3 times, but instead of stopping, they saw the *Gift* continue to sail off and out of sight.

Once the formalities were dealt with and the payment made for the passengers' release, the *Mary and John* also departed. They followed the same route but the *Gift*, a smaller ship was also a faster ship and the two were not to be joined again. Their hope was there that they would encounter each other somewhere along the way. They kept their course westward according to the planned route as much as the wind and weather would permit.

In reflecting back to two evenings ago, when they had the skirmish with the Dutch, one issue continued to plague James. Captain Hartman made the statement that Spanish spies were common among all the vessels traveling to the New World. In their case, it was because of that spy their ship had traveled into Spanish Territory. If for no other reason, a spy could be used to gather information about those on board, discover otherwise "sensitive" information from communications to England, or to gather information about their future fort: how many houses, location of the storehouse or arsenal.

"Do we have a spy among us?" James wondered, "If so, would I be able to spot him? I'll have to keep an eye out."

During the next 26 days at sea, they only saw one sail. From its flag, they determined that the ship was from Salcombe, England, a village on the Devon Coast. The weather had been accommodating for the most part with just a few, small storms along the way. On the morning of July 27, they finally sounded and saw they were approaching the coast.

Then they fished and took in a plentiful catch of nearly 100 very large Codfish. Continuing along the coast, the wind being southwest, they set their sails west by northwest toward the mainland. The coast was full of islands and broken ground. Finally, at 3 o'clock in the afternoon of the last day of July, they anchored at an island for the night.

They no sooner dropped anchor when they saw a Biscayne shallop (small wooden boat) approaching. The men drew their firearms, not knowing what to expect. As it came closer, they could see it had four natives on board; three men and one young lad. If there had been any question before, it was now obvious these islands were indeed inhabited by natives. Whether they were pleasant or aggressive was yet to be seen. It was as if this boat's mission was to determine if the new visitors were friendly or not. They wanted to appear less aggressive by having a young lad visible at the helm. No bows and arrows were drawn and they purposefully would not come too close to appear to be too aggressive. The shallop circled the *Mary and John* while the entire crew and passengers watched.

Captain Robert told his men to drop their firearms to

their sides, showing the natives that they did not feel threatened.

James commented to his brother Robert, "Where do you suppose these natives got a Biscayne shallop? Is it stolen?"

"Good question, brother. Perhaps it was stolen, but I have heard that the Basques occasionally make fishing alliances with the Micmac Indians, giving them vessels as this one, in exchange for being able to fish without being harmed. From all indications, I suspect that is the case here," Robert concluded.

James was once again amazed at his brother's knowledge of the practices at sea. He wondered if he could ever live up to be the leader his brother was. He looked forward to the opportunity of being the Commander of the new fort to see if these skills came as easy for him as they were for his brother Robert.

The shallop circled the ship and then headed off around the bend of the island.

Confident that no one was in danger, once again the crew fished and encountered another huge catch of Codfish, but this time, they also caught a supply of the largest lobsters ever seen by anyone on board the *Mary and John*.

They were bringing their traps up when the shallop returned with 5 canoes. This time, the shallop no longer carried the child but someone who was obviously their chief. Commander Gilbert looked at them as their leader focused on Gilbert, and much to everyone's surprise, shouting up to him said, "Bonjour!"

No one expected the Micmac Indian to speak French. Commander Gilbert however was able to communicate with him since he learned the language while studying at university. Everyone was anxious to know what the leader was saying.

"He says his name is Sabodina. He says he learned the language of the white men when trading with them. He said he wants to come aboard and negotiate a trade but is concerned for his safety and is asking us to send someone over the side to stay with his men while he is with us." Gilbert translated. He looked at Captain Robert and James for affirmation. "What do you think? Can we trust him?"

Together, they assumed all would be well, since it was an even trade. So, they lowered one of their apprentices, Wilson, into the shallop while Sabodina climbed aboard carrying a bag full of what looked like skins. The shallop along with all of the other canoes quickly departed hurrying up the coast.

Commander Gilbert instructed one of his men to get the chest they had stored full of items used for trade. Once it arrived, Gilbert opened it, showing a store of knives, beads, and jewelry. Sabodina in turn, pulled some worthless beaver skins from his bag and laid them next to the chest. Gilbert, Robert and James examined the skins and concluded they were of no value.

Commander Gilbert asked Sabodina in French what he was attempting to do. Sabodina looked fiercely into the commander's eyes and told him that the last time the French traded with him, his brother was brutally killed and he swore that he would get revenge on the next white man he encountered. Now, one of their men would be brutally killed. After that he howled a vicious war cry, startling everyone, grabbed one of the knives from the chest and jumped overboard. He began swimming towards the beach.

Captain James immediately jumped overboard after Sabodina. Three other men did the same, followed by Commander Gilbert and ten of his men in the ship's longboat. James had his eye on the native and followed him ashore, chasing him into the brush.

Sabodina had his bow and arrows stashed in the bushes just above the beach and was making his way towards them when James tackled him and brought him to the ground. They fought intensely. This was one of those times when James was glad he had trained so masterfully. As he turned, the native freed himself from James' hold, pulled the knife and stood up to challenge James face to face, slowly backing up towards his bow in the bushes. James pulled his knife as well and the two were at a stand off, when the other three men arrived to show their support for James. This made Sabodina more defensive but still backing up towards the bushes. James saw the corner of the bow sticking out of the bush. He knew he had to keep the native from getting his weapon.

At this point, Commander Gilbert arrived, his men armed with their firearms. "Perhaps we can reason with him James."

"Reason with him? Look at him. It would be easier to reason with a wildcat!" James huffed.

"If we do not try, we will never see young Wilson again. I think it is the only way," retorted Gilbert.

He spoke to Sabodina in French, "We are not French, Sabodina! We are English! Let's talk this through, so no one gets hurt." Gilbert paused and attempted to look calm and in control.

"You can see, you are outnumbered by my men. They have muskets and if we wanted to harm you, we could, but we came to make peace in a new world. I'm sorry for the loss of your brother, but we weren't the ones responsible for his death, the French are. We are English."

Sabodina thought about what was being said. He realized all that Commander Gilbert had said was true. He must truly want a peaceable outcome or he himself would be dead by now.

"Come on, Sabodina, put your knife down, give us back our man, and we will both depart from here without any bloodshed." Gilbert said.

The native tossed his knife on the beach. After a moment of maintaining his defense mode, he dropped his hands into a defenseless fashion. The English lowered their weapons as well while James grabbed the bow and arrows from the bush.

"I will bring the young man back to your ship." Sabodina said in French. "He is unharmed. I'm sure of it."

"No," Commander Gilbert replied, "We will go with you to insure his safety. If he has been harmed, you can be assured, things will not end up peaceably."

They followed Sabodina on a trail into the woods and soon came upon the Micmac village. The village was full of wigwams made of saplings of spruce, lashed together at the top and then covered with birch bark. Each one could house roughly 12 natives. To walk into the village with their chief caused a bit of an uproar.

The young apprentice Wilson was tied up outside of the first visible wigwam. Surrounded by a dozen natives with their bows drawn in preparation for a command from their chief.

"Lower your bows!" Sabodina instructed them firmly in their language. They lowered their weapons. "Set him free!"

They untied the sailor. Then, the chief walked over to him and led him back to Gilbert, James, and the crew.

Leaving the chief there, they all quietly walked down the path back to the longboat, grateful to have the young apprentice alive and unharmed. Then, they rowed back to the

Mary and John, hoisted the anchor and bid good riddance to the island and its inhabitants.

When James arrived in his cabin, he placed Sabodina's bow and arrow in his sea chest. He would retain it as a reminder of how aggressive the natives of the New World could be.

It had been a while since James wrote in his *Relation of a Voyage to Sagadahoc*. There had been many repetitive days at sea when nothing notable had occurred. Not so today. James had a memorable day for sure. He prayed a prayer of thanksgiving for today's outcome of events, then prayed for Rachel before logging in today's events in the journal.

The weather was permitting through the night. The first day of August in 1607 proved to be a lovely day with lots of summer sunshine, and beautiful vistas of the coastline. Captain James couldn't help but rehearse in his mind the events from just the night before. Had he not jumped overboard after the chief, he would have gotten away and they would never have seen the young apprentice Wilson

alive again. Surely, this one event will boost James'
reputation and respect level amongst his crew, passengers,
and his girl, Rachel, when she reads about it in his journal.
But, enough about the past, this morning, all James cared
about was enjoying the sunshine as he made his rounds upon
the ship. Now, he looked forward to the next adventure,
whatever that may be.

On Friday, August 7th, the *Mary and John* had come
upon another island. They surmised the island was St.
George Island.

St. George Island was one of the islands noted in
Captain George Weymouth's expedition two years earlier.
He planted a cross there and claimed the right of the land for
the English. Now as they approached, they became even
more excited when they saw a ship's sail in the harbor. As
they neared, they could see it was the *Gift of God*! She was
waiting for the *Mary and John* to arrive as Captain James and
Master Martin had previously discussed before leaving Santa
Cruz.

The reunion was great, ending with a feast and celebration on the *Mary and John*. James rejoiced over seeing his friends, Commander Popham, the preacher Seymour, and Skidwarres alive and well.

About midnight, with the weather being fair and the wind being calm, Captain Gilbert, James, Robert, Skidwarres and ten others boarded the ship's boat and rowed west among many gallant islands and found the Pemaquid River. Skidwarres stood at the front of the boat and by his direction, they landed in a little cove and marched over the neck of land for nearly three miles until arriving at a group of savage houses that were uninhabited.

"Village gone. No longer here." Skidwarres commented in his broken English. "No family. English go back to ship now."

James observed Skidwarres was showing obvious concern and reluctance about leading the English to his family.

"Don't be uncomfortable with us being here, Skiddy,"

James said. "Let me assure you we think of you as one of us. We mean no harm to your people."

"We refuse to depart until we have an opportunity to speak to some of them," commented Captain Gilbert.

After a while, he reluctantly brought them to another habitation where there were nearly a hundred men, women, and children. The Chief Commander was none other than Dehanada, the interpreter who was left the year before by Captain Pring.

When the Indians caught sight of the Englishmen, they began a loud howling or cry, which made everyone present assemble with bows and arrows drawn. It appeared to be another standoff. The Englishmen made a stand though and asked the Indians to come near them.

Then, Skidwarres addressed them in their native language, showing them who they were. "Skidwarres? Is that you?" inquired a surprised Dehanada.

When Dehanada perceived it was Skidwarres, he convinced them all to lay down their weapons, came and embraced him and the Englishmen. The Indians welcomed the Englishmen into their houses and there, they spoke for over two hours learning more about their culture.

At the close of their visit, Dehanada pulled Skidwarres aside so no one could hear him. "Stay with us, Brother. We are your people. You are not English. This is your land."

He could see Skidwarres was conflicted in his emotions. He was truly remorseful about leaving but he decided to lead the group on the trek back to their boats. "I will see you again soon," he assured Dehanada.

They departed and arrived back to the ship on Saturday afternoon.

The next morning being Sunday, August 9th, the entirety of both ships met at the cross on the island and Rev. Seymour delivered a sermon giving thanks to God for our happy meeting and safe arrival into the country.

Early Monday morning, Commander Popham in his shallop with thirty others and Commander Gilbert in his ship's boat with another twenty men, sailed towards the Pemaquid River again. Skidwarres and Captain James were with the group. They came up the river to where the Indian's houses were. When Dehanada and the other Indians spotted them, they drew their bows and arrows and met them on the sandy beach.

Skidwarres spoke to them as well as the Englishmen to try to comfort their fears of such a large group arriving. But Dehanada refused to allow all of them to come ashore. The English did not want to offend Dehanada, so only twelve of the most important people of the group came ashore and talked for a while. After a while, they were content to have the rest of the party come ashore as well. They purposed to be as kind as they possibly could. Never the less, after about an hour, all of the natives suddenly stood and left walking into the woods.

The English perceived their time with the natives had been productive in establishing a friendship with the tribe and a possible trading enterprise with them. But now, it was time to depart. Skidwarres decided he wanted to stay with his people. He came to Captain James.

"Skidwarres want to stay here. You go." He told James as he pointed to the boat.

"Promise me, you'll come back and stay with us, Skiddy," James told him. "We still need you to help guide us and interpret for us. But we won't take you by force. You've been a faithful member of our expedition. Take the time you need."

Skidwarres promised to return to them the next day, so he stayed with the Indians.

Two days later, Skidwarres still hadn't returned to the ship so they weighed their anchors and set sail to what would be at their final destination at the Sagadahoc.

James and Rev. Seymour reflected upon the young Pemaquid Indian, Skidwarres, and all of the experiences they had been through with him at their side.

"I trust that Skiddy will enjoy his future with his people. I will miss him tremendously," remarked the preacher as he held the rail and watched the shore of this amazing land.

"We all will, Richard. We all will!" James said. He placed his hand on top of the preacher's and patted it in agreement.

CHAPTER SIX

Construction Begins

It was Sunday afternoon on August 16, 1607 when the two ships finally anchored side by side in the River Sagadahoc. The weather was calm and they were all filled with excitement that they had finally reached their destination after seventy-seven days of journey.

The crew and passengers met on the *Mary and John* for a Sunday sermon by Richard Seymer. Once again, the preacher prayed a prayer of thanksgiving for them having arrived safely, a prayer for Sir John Popham who was financing the expedition, and a prayer for direction and leading of the Lord to show them exactly where to plant their colony. Many of them were planters or colonists who hoped to ship timber back to England, to find gold, silver, and other valuable minerals, and to establish a fur trade with the local natives. Much to the concern of some of the leaders, there were only a few farmers who could actually plant crops to help replenish the food supplies.

After the sermon, once again Alfred, Edgar, and Henry entertained the crew and passengers with their music while they all enjoyed the summer sunlight and mugs of beer.

Commander George Popham called a meeting with Commander Raleigh Gilbert, Captain Ellis, Captain Robert Davis, and his brother, Captain James Davis.

"Tomorrow, early in the morning, we will begin our search for the most convenient place to construct our plantation for the Crown," reported Popham. "I will take thirty of our planters and our preacher in my shallop and head up the river."

Gilbert also reported, "And Captain James and I shall take eighteen more with us in my ship's boat, including our carpenters, to spy out the river and help decide upon a location as well. We will leave Captain Robert here to manage those left on board."

"We shall depart at the break of dawn, so join the celebration but be sure to get some rest," Popham concluded.

The next morning the two boats sailed up into the Sagadahoc River nearly 14 leagues. They found the river to be most gallant, very broad at times, and of a good depth: Definitely suitable for the ships to travel. The river was impressive to say the least, with sturgeon leaping above the water on each side of the boats as they sailed along. After a while, they went ashore and refreshed themselves with fresh water and fruit growing in abundance. Then, about 9:00 in the evening, they turned to return to their ships, arriving the next day at about 2:00 in the afternoon.

James located his brother Robert and reported what they had determined about the voyage. "We found this river to be very pleasant, with many good islands in it and being wide, deep, and with many creeks branching from it. After much discussion, we've determined where to construct our plantation. Not too far from here is the very mouth of the River Sagadahoc. On the west side of the river, there is a piece of land that is almost an island in and of itself. It is of great size and will be the prefect place. "

Robert was in favor of the location. "It sounds like it will work. I can't wait until I get to see it for myself."

At this time, James brought up one concern he had, "While we were on the shore, three canoes full of natives came slowly past us, examining us very closely, then rowed up the river and out of sight. What do you suppose they were doing, brother?"

"Hopefully, they are friendly and only wanted to make sure that we were also. The fact that we didn't ready ourselves for battle probably showed them we could be trusted. Perhaps we can establish a good trading relationship with them." Robert said.

They all went ashore to the location selected. The men had placed a cross in the ground on the bank where the settlement would be constructed. Reverend Richard Seymour brought his Bible and Book of Common Prayer with him, delivered a sermon, and sanctified the ground with all of them present. At of the end of the sermon, the *Patent of the Colony* was read by George Popham; formally explaining the orders and laws prescribed. Then, the leaders assembled for the inauguration of the officers of the new colony.

"As the representative of Almighty God," Rev. Seymour declared, "I would like to recognize and swear in those who are called to lead our new Plantation. When I call your name, please come forth and kneel before the cross."

"Sir George Popham, President of the colony." Seymour waited for each individual to come forth, remove their hats, and kneel at the front of the group.

"Captain Raleigh Gilbert, Admiral and 2nd in command"

"Edward Harlow, Master of the Ordinance."

"Captain Robert Davis, Sergeant Major."

"Captain Ellis Best, Marshall and Keeper of the Peace."

"Sir Leaman, Secretary and Documenter"

"Mr. Gome Carew, Chief Searcher."

"And finally Captain James Davis, Captain of the Fort."

Then, the preacher opened his Bible and read to those kneeling.

"The Holy Word of God instructs us in the Book of James, Chapter 1, verse 5: *If any of you lack wisdom, let him ask of God, which giveth to all men liberally, and reproacheth no man, and it shall be given him. But let him ask in faith, and waiver not: for he that wavereth is like a wave of the sea, tossed of the wind, and carried away. Neither let that man think that he shall receive anything from the Lord.* I trust that each of you, realize that you are here by design of Almighty God, Himself. We are mere humans and when you have need of wisdom, you will draw upon God and His Holy Spirit, to give you that wisdom. You are never alone."

That being said, Seymer closed his Bible and placed it on the bolder next to the cross.

"With the authority given to me by Almighty God

and as Representative of His Highness, James, King of England, I hereby commission each of you to your assigned positions of this settlement."

With all of them kneeling before the cross, Rev. Richard Seymer laid his hands upon each of their heads individually as he pronounced a blessing upon them. After which, the planters and members of the crew congratulated them and returned to their ships for the remainder of the night.

Captain James was tired but invigorated by the day's events. It was official now. He was to be the captain of the new fort once they began building it. He came from a family of well-known and high-ranking captains and now his chance had come to show his family and friends that he, himself had what it takes to have such a high ranking.

Before closing his eyes for sleep, he pulled out the journal given to him by his love, Rachel. "I have much to tell you, my love," he thought to himself. He held the book in his hands, closed his eyes and remembered her beautiful smile and red hair. Then, he prayed for her, found his pen and began logging in the day's events.

The next morning proved to be a special day because ground was to be broken, beginning construction of the new Fort St George. It was to be named after the patron Saint of England. One of the colonists, John Hunt, the official draughtsman of the colony, had drawn a detailed plan of the fort. It was to be a star-shaped bastion, which included several defensive walls in which to house the cannons. The structure would be large enough to contain a number of houses, including the Admiral's house, a chapel, a storehouse, a cooperage, and a guardhouse.

All of the leaders stood in a line along the location of the first wall. President Popham stuck his shovel in the ground and turned the first scoop of dirt, followed by all of the others. Fort St. George officially began. This was Thursday, August 20, 1607.

The company labored hard all day digging trenches with pick and shovel.

One of the company, an experienced shipwright by the name of Master Digby of London, had been given the charge to build a small 30 ton ship called a pinnace, using the natural resources at hand. This ship would be heralded as the first one fully constructed in the new world. It would be titled the *Virginia*. Digby, along with some of his experienced carpenters, located a favorable spot on the river where construction could begin on the vessel. The plan was to have both the Fort and the *Virginia* completed at the same time.

"What a proud day it will be," President Popham declared to Admiral Gilbert, "to announce to the investors of the Plymouth Company that not only was Fort St. George completed but also the very first ship constructed in the New World."

"She must be built stout enough to carry heavy cargoes of furs, fish, and metals back to England," stated Admiral Gilbert. "There is a small forest of oak trees up the coast a bit that would be perfect to use. I must tell Digby about it."

The men labored hard on the fort under the direction of Captain James and John Hunt, digging trenches in the hard soil, cutting and nailing logs to fortify the walls. The first building to to complete was to be a storehouse so supplies could be permanently unloaded from the *Gift of God* and the *Mary and John*.

Two weeks had gone by and construction was coming along well. Now that the ships were no longer at sea, Captain James began to notice a polarizing of affection for the two main leaders of the colony; President Popham and Admiral Gilbert, who was second in command. Those who had been on Popham's vessel felt an allegiance to him and similarly those of Gilbert's vessel. The men were not used to having two men with such strong leadership tactics giving orders, sometimes even contradicting each other's.

As the men worked hard on the fort, sweating in the late summer heat, James had to call upon Captain Ellis, the new Marshal, to be more present to break up small fights and arguments among them.

On the following Saturday, being September 6, the lookout spotted something on the river. "Natives!" he shouted, while reaching for his firearm and shooting in the air to signal to those working on the fort and the *Virginia*.

Captain James ran to the lookout point to assist the guard.

"There appears to be nine canoes full of Indians and they are coming this way!" the guard fearfully informed the Captain. "What shall we do sir?"

As the canoes neared the shore, James could see the canoes were full of men, women, and children, roughly forty to be counted. He looked through his spyglass and to his surprise, he saw his old friend, Skidwarres, standing in one canoe and Dehanada in the other. He quickly fetched Rev. Seymour and ran to welcome the canoes. When the other men saw their friend, Skiddy, they dropped their tools and ran to greet him as well!

"Skiddy, we thought we would never see you again!" exclaimed Seymour.

"It's great to see you again, to see that you are in good health. What brings you here today?" Captain James asked.

Skidwarres replied in his broken English, "Captain, after our clash with Dutch, and you show me how much you are part my family, I said you will meet Skidwarres' family. Well, here they are. Me keep promise."

James was overwhelmed with compassion for Skidwarres and his family. The native motioned to those behind him for them to come closer to him. Three young boys approached James and Skidwarres. He gave them instruction in his native tongue and they put their arms out as if to shake hands. Skidwarres smiled.

"These my brothers. Pelano, Debano, and Skiharo." James and Richard shook their hands but pulled them close for an embrace as well.

"This my mother. Skidwarres no longer have father." James and Richard extended their hands to her as well.

Skidwarres then focused on Rev. Seymour and said,

99

"Skidwarres Christian. Dehanada Christian. Skidwarres' family want to be Christian too. Will you teach them?"

"Nothing would thrill me more!" answered the preacher. "Will you interpret for me?"

Skidwarres nodded.

"Let's go sit on the beach over there."

Some others joined the preacher and Skidwarres as they walked to the beach. There was a large boulder there where both Skidwarres and Richard could sit side by side to address the crowd.

Captain James addressed Dehanada, "Are you hungry? Ready for some good English food?" The cooks had already increased their portions to accommodate the crowd joining them for lunch. All were well fed.

James and Dehanada sat alone, talking about the new settlement and pulled information from him as how to handle the natives living nearby.

"Occasionally, we have seen canoes go by but have not been able to connect with them. Do you think you can help us establish trade with those up the river from us, here?" James inquired.

Suddenly, there was a roar of shouting and cheers behind them and they could see the preacher and Skidwarres in the water baptizing his new converts into their Christian faith.

Dehanada responded, "I can introduce you to the Bashabe, who is the chief commander of these parts. Much like your president Popham is the chief commander of your plantation. If he chooses to trust you and begin trading, it will be up to him. It might be difficult to persuade him though. He has seen too many agreements made with those from Europe fail, but it has generally been the Spanish and French who have not kept their word."

"That would satisfy our needs, Dehanada!"

The fellowshipping continued until nighttime, when the natives withdrew in their canoes to the other side of the river. Skidwarres stayed a while longer sharing what could be one of the last times being with his English friends. When the darkness settled in good, he needed to return to his people, so Admiral Gilbert, Captain Ellis and James took him on their boat to his company on the other side of the river. The three men stayed overnight there until the morning, at which time they departed in their canoes to the river Pemaquid. Before leaving, they promised to meet the next day and lead Admiral Gilbert and the others to the river Penobskott and to where the Bashabe lived.

The next day, Gilbert, James, Ellis, and 20 others loaded their boat full of merchandise to trade with the Bashabe. They planned to meet Skidwarres and Dehanada at the Pemaquid River before the trek farther up the coastline but a storm arose, keeping them from meeting at the arranged time. The storm lasted for three full days. It wasn't until Friday that they were able to depart and meet at the proposed location. When they arrived, there was no one to be found, so they attempted to find the Penobskott River on their own. They sailed for the next five days but could not find the river or their friends, so they returned to the fort and to business as usual.

Finally, after another week of hard work, two canoes appeared at the beach. Skidwarres and Dehanada, brought with them two natives: one was the Bashabe's brother and the other was another leader of the tribe on the Penobskott River, named Amenguin. President Popham showed them much kindness, fed them, and invited them to stay overnight.

The next morning was Sunday and Popham invited them to attend church services in their newly constructed Fort St. George Chapel. They participated with much reverence and silence as Dehanada acted as their interpreter of what was said.

This was a day of rest for those at the fort, so the men seized the opportunity to once again play the game, *Hubbub*, taught them by Skidwarres. While the game was being played, trade negotiations were being made with Dehanada translating. All appeared to be going well and after dinner they departed. Popham gave each of them copper beads and knives, which made them very happy. He presented a special gift to the Bashabe's brother as a gesture to show the natives that trading with those at the Fort was going to be very lucrative for both sides.

The next morning the governing body assembled in the Chapel to take stock of their progress.

"The members and investors of our colony need to know the state of our affairs here," President Popham stated, "They need to be encouraged that their money has been used wisely, all is well, and their finances are indeed going to return tremendous return for them. It has been nearly five months since we departed and we need to send a ship back to give them an update of our success. I suggest that Captain Robert Davis, along with a minimum crew, sail the *Mary and John* while the weather is still permitting."

Admiral Gilbert then added his concern. "Mr. President, I agree that we need to send the *Mary and John* back to England, but not for the purpose you're suggesting. It appears you wish for your uncle, Sir John, to know how successful you are at commanding this post, but the fact is we have not yet proven our success. The expectation was for us to find precious minerals, gold, silver, copper, and strike up a robust trade with the natives so our investors would show a quick profit; all this of course, in competition with the southern colony of Jamestown. Truth is, our metallurgist has not found such metals and we have not produced a benefit of trade more than a few beaver skins, and poor quality at that!"

Gilbert was getting passionate in his voice and some of the leadership disagreements the two have had along the way were beginning to finally surface. All eyes were focused on him as he continued.

"I suggest that the *Mary and John* return alright, but mainly for the supplies needed to keep our fort sustainable. So far, all we have seen that this land has to offer is loads of fish and great timber. But we are now approaching winter, and because of our late arrival, we could not plant any crops to harvest. If we send Captain Davis back now, we may be able to have fresh supplies before the roughest weather hits."

Everyone agreed the need to send the *Mary and John*

back for supplies was an urgent need and essential to their success.

"I will ready my crew and depart immediately." Captain Robert Davis replied to the men. He arose and left the room. His brother James was right behind him.

"I will help you get ready brother. I am sure you can use it." James said.

"Thank you. You've been the Master of the ship, so I'm confident you know what we need to depart." The two immediately began gathering a crew and supplies.

The *Mary and John* was ready to depart the next day. The weather was amiable, a bit of clouds off on the horizon, but otherwise all appeared well.

James approached Captain Robert with a letter. "President Popham asked me to give you this letter to his Uncle, Sir John. He said it would assist you in getting the supplies we need. There is also a drawing of the fort here, drawn by Mr. Hunt."

"Have a safe journey, Robert! May God be with

you!" James said.

Captain Robert and his crew bid their farewells and departed for England. The day was Tuesday, October 7, 1607.

CHAPTER SEVEN

Winter Arrives!

The *Mary and John*, captained by Robert Davis, approached the Lizard Peninsula and its Lighthouse on December 1, 1607. The journey from Fort St. George had been uneventful but long. Robert knew it was just a matter of hours before they would be arriving at Plymouth Harbor. As much as he loved the sea, he was anxious to set his feet on the Devon shore once again and see his family and friends. The crew readied the ship for its arrival.

Robert stood on deck at the rail watching the familiar English shoreline go by. Anthony, his Ship's Master was standing next to him. "I can't help but wonder how those left behind at the Fort are fairing," commented Anthony. "At least we know they won't starve from lack of fish! I've never seen fish in that abundance before, Captain."

"Nor I, Anthony." He paused for a moment. "Our arrival will be a surprise to all. Anthony, I don't know much about your family. Are they from Devon or Plymouth?"

"Oh no, Sir. My family is not from around here, so I have no one to look up when we arrive. I'm not like you, Sir," Anthony stated, "without doubt, the Davis Family will be glad to see you're home safe. What are your plans, Captain?"

Robert thought about it for a moment, then said, "I've got to submit a letter and a drawing of Fort St. George to Sir John Popham first thing, to request the needed supplies and the finances required to purchase them. Then, off to see my mother and father."

Anthony looked surprised. "A drawing? You mean to tell me you have a drawing of the new fort with you? I didn't know one existed. Tell me about it, Captain."

"Come with me to my cabin and I'll show it to you." Robert and Anthony walked back up to his cabin and Robert pulled a rolled sheet of parchment from his bag and laid it on his desk. "It was drawn by our Draughtsman, Mr. Hunt. Did a stellar job, don't you think? It details everything we've built so far: the star-shaped walls that contain the cannons, the houses the storehouse, even the chapel. I believe his nephew, Sir George, is banking on his uncle John seeing the progress we've made so far and as a result, he'll be able to keep his investors happy as well."

The noise, laughter and commands being shouted, outside of the cabin grew louder as the men prepared to drop anchor. "I must tend to my duties, Captain! We've arrived at Plymouth Harbor." Anthony hurried outside and soon Captain Davis followed to make sure all was in order with the Customs Officer and other harbor authorities.

Afterwards, Captain Davis gathered his cloak, hat and a few other items from his cabin. He was preparing to depart from the ship when he remembered he left the letter and drawing in his quarters. He retrieved the letter, but when he went to his desk to collect the drawing, it was not there. He looked all around the cabin to no avail. "This is peculiar," he thought to himself, "If this drawing were to get into the hands of the Spanish or French, they would know Fort St. George in explicit detail. Perhaps, Anthony has it. I'll ask him." He went on a search for Anthony around the vessel but could not locate him. He asked the seaman at the top of the plank leading to the dock.

"Have you seen Master Anthony?"

"Yes Sir, he left rather abruptly down the plank a while back without making much contact with others, got in a carriage and rode off," the seaman said.

Robert sat down on a barrel and threw his hands up to his forehead. "Anthony must have taken the drawing from my desk," he thought to himself, "How could I have been so foolish as to let him see the thing in the first place? What purpose would he have to take it? I wonder if he is a spy? If so, for whom...the Spanish? The French?"

After a few minutes of regret, he composed himself, gathered his items once again and left ship. He got on a carriage and gave the command for the driver to take him to the Davis estate in Devon.

His father was sitting at his desk when he heard his wife welcoming someone at the door. Before he could get out of his chair, the door sprang open and there was his son, Robert greeting him with his bearded smile! "Father! I'm back!" The two embraced enthusiastically and then Robert sat down on his couch and gave an update of what had happened at the new Fort St. George.

"So, I need to get this message to Sir John Popham," Robert said as he held up the letter written by George, "to get things in order for purchasing our needed supplies."

"You don't know, do you Robert?" Sir Thomas said, "John Popham died just ten days after you left Plymouth Harbor on your expedition. He went to bed after a meeting with his investors and his heart just stopped. His servant found him unconscious in his bed. "

"John Popham as you know, was the driving force behind the investors of the Plymouth Company of Virginia. So, when he passed away, the investors lost interest in the colony, assuming you were never to be seen again. Let me see the letter, son."

Thomas quickly read the letter.

"Oh my! This letter explains how successful the Popham Colony is! I believe once the investors see this, they'll get back on board. We must get it to them, but I might suggest, nothing would be more valuable than you personally bringing it to them. You can give them a first-hand account of your experiences. We can go together if you wish. I can arrange meetings with the major investors."

"Thank you Father. There is one person I'd like to get hold of before any of that though: Rachel Keyes. I think she would like to know the progress of the colony and of course the condition of James, if you understand what I mean." Robert said with a smile.

"Ah, Rachel," Thomas sighed, "such a beautiful young lady and beautiful heart! Since your departure, she has visited our family nearly every Sunday after church services. She brings us treats that she has baked herself and offers prayers for James, you, and the colony. She has won our hearts. If my summation is correct, your brother truly has found the right woman for a future wife."

"I agree indeed, Father. She is practically all he wants to talk about when you are alone with him. Perhaps she would consider visiting the investors with me as well. They might say no to me, but how could they possibly say no to such a beautiful young lady, impassioned the way she is?"

As a result, Robert contacted Rachel and the two of them, working with Thomas' direction, began soliciting aid from past investors. It was a very slow process, yet proving to be very successful.

Meanwhile, back at Fort St. George, the past two months were mixed with positive and negative. The climate was changing drastically, as it does in the Northwest Atlantic. Fall leaves were enjoyed for a mere short while before they were replaced with early snowstorms. The days were now short and the cold nights long. The fort itself was now complete after much hard work from the planters.

Supplies however were being rationed as they awaited the return of the *Mary and John* around February.

The most difficult obstacle James was facing in his command of Fort St. George was keeping moral high. President Popham was beginning to show obvious discomfort in his physical body as the weather changed. He complained of aches and pains in his joints that were being aggravated by the cold weather. He stayed focused around the fort and occupied his time encouraging the builders and carpenters who were completing the fort and the new pinnace, *Virginia*.

Admiral Raleigh Gilbert on the other hand continued to pursue trade with the local natives, traveling up the rivers and through oak forests as the weather permitted. He had a large following of adventurous young men looking for action and excitement in the new country. As a result, allegiance between Admiral Gilbert and the men of the colony continued to grow while allegiance between President Popham and the men was beginning to deteriorate. This only grew worse as the men became more disturbed by the need to ration their supplies.

When the first day of December arrived, the Sagadahoc was hit with a blizzard which brought five feet of snow with it. Fortunately, Admiral Gilbert and his men were at the fort regrouping when it hit. All trade was suspended and everyone did all they could to stay warm and safe inside of the fort.

After three days, James and Captain Ellis were making their rounds in the blizzard, checking the security of all buildings and their inhabitants, when they heard a ruckus happening in the large meeting room.

"I haven't seen so many men in such tight quarters since we were onboard ship!" Captain Ellis had just remarked to James as they neared the building.

Inside, the men had taken sides. The ones who had been exploring and trading with Gilbert were on one side and those who had built the fort were on the other.

"If it hadn't been for our hard work building this very building, you would be out in the snow you thankless buzzards! We deserve to have a greater portion of rations than you!" shouted the fort's blacksmith as he raised his hammer in anger.

"Well, if we weren't out there, making friends with the natives, you would be fighting a war rather than the weather! We deserve a greater portion than you!" responded one of Gilbert's crew. He pushed the blacksmith in the chest, knocking him backwards into the arms of his friends.

"This is getting out of hand!" Captain Ellis said to James as he rushed into the room and the center of the action. He blew his whistle to command attention while James placed himself between the two men, holding them from throwing blows.

"Look, gentlemen, unless you want to be thrown into the brig, you'll calm down!" James said. "You're not in an English pub. You are representing the Crown, so act civil!"

With that, the men paused and turned away. "You are correct, Sir. I don't know what has gotten into me," said the blacksmith. "Aye. Me neither" responded Gilbert's man.

One of the other planters shouted from the crowd, "Look, it was bad enough that we arrived so late in the season that we couldn't plant any crops. Now we didn't plan correctly and are short of supplies. The winter has set in and it's colder than we've ever experienced before!"

"Aye, and now even all of the creeks and smaller rivers have frozen over!" said another man. "Even the trade with the natives has stopped!"

"I'm ready to call it quits! It's over for me!" shouted another.

"Aye! I didn't sign on for this! If we don't do something, we're going to starve to death!" others said, "I don't want to die in this frozen wilderness!"

"Unless the *Mary and John* comes with supplies soon, we won't last until spring. There's not enough food to go around!"

"You're the Captain of Fort St. George. What shall we do?" they asked James. "Yeah, what shall we do? "

"Let me ponder that question, men." James said, "and

I'll get back to you soon." He paused, " In the meanwhile, please sit still."

The next morning, James had a meeting with Admiral Gilbert, President Popham, Rev. Seymour, and Captain Ellis.

"I've thought through what the men were complaining about last night and I think the only solution is to allow some of the men to return home. They've lost vision and are miserable. I'm proposing that we load up the *Gift of God* and make the journey home," James suggested.

"How many do you suppose need to depart, Captain?" asked the preacher Seymour.

"There is only room for forty-five men on board besides the crew," answered James.

"Who would captain the ship back to England?" asked Popham.

"I navigated the *Gift* for most of the way here. I could do it if you are all in agreement with that," answered James. "My duties could be divided up amongst you all here, especially since we are so restricted due to the weather."

They all cast their vote as a *YES*.

Rev. Seymour spoke up. "I would like to suggest something first, friends. This is a serious decision. It means a setback for the plans of the plantation of the Popham Colony. You asked me to weigh in on the decision, so I would like to ask for you to give it a few days before solidifying or announcing the decision to take half of the colonists back to England."

All eyes were upon the preacher. "I agree that it appears this is the only solution but an anxious mind in an exhausted body can lead to a terrible decision."

Seymour opened his Bible at that point. "Let me read something to you, Gentlemen, from the Apostle Paul in his letter to the church in Philippi: *Be anxious for nothing; but in everything by prayer and supplication, with thanksgiving, let your requests be made known unto God. And the peace of God, which passeth all understanding, shall keep your hearts and minds though Christ Jesus.*" Seymour closed his book and looked at the men.

"We can always count on you, preacher, to keep us on the right path" said President Popham. "Let's give it three days and if we feel the same at that time, we will announce our plan and begin making preparation."

The weather conditions intensified even more over the next three days while the men were cooped up in their cabins with nothing to do. Finally Captain James told his friends, "The sooner we do this, the better! The men are ready to kill each other!"

They all agreed and a meeting was called in the chapel.

"Gentlemen, as President I must inform you of a decision we have made. We have run extremely low on supplies and have decided to allow some of you to return to England. The fort is completed so this is as good of a time as any to complete that part of the charter. Captain James Davis will navigate the *Gift of God*. There is room for forty-five men plus the crew to depart with him. Admiral Gilbert and I will command the settlement here in his absence. Speak up if you wish to return with Captain James."

Quickly, hands began being raised. "I wish to go," one said. "So do I, Count me in," said some others. Sir Leaman, the Secretary and Documenter of the colony officially logged all forty-five spaces as filled.

Master Digby, the shipwright, raised his hand and said, "My team and I wish to stay and complete our project! It won't be long before our pretty little boat will be done. We would have it finished by now, had it not been for the weather. We may not be great at farming, or mining, but one thing we will be known as are excellent ship builders! This ship, the *Virginia*, will be the very first English ship built in America and we can be proud of that for sure!"

Captain James addressed the crowd. "Weather and wind permitting, we shall depart by noon tomorrow. We will meet at the longboats in the morning. Enjoy your last day at Sagadahoc men, and tonight, we'll celebrate one last time, all of us together! We have plenty of beer and plenty of fish!"

President George Popham wrote another letter to give

to his uncle, Sir John Popham upon their arrival back at Plymouth. This time, he wrote it in Latin, so no one could read it if it fell into someone else's hands. His uncle had taught him Latin as a young boy and it had been a usual routine for them to communicate in such a manner. He gave the letter to Captain James for safe keeping.

As James thought about the trip back to England, he couldn't help but get excited when thinking about seeing Miss Rachel Keyes. He had been faithfully documenting each event along the way in the journal she gave him. He anticipated seeing her expression as she reads about their adventures.

On December 16, 1607, the *Gift of God* was loaded with forty-five planters and ten crew members, equaling 55 men and leaving 65 to continue at Fort St. George.

James said his goodbyes to those left with the promise of immediately returning with needed supplies. He specifically searched out Reverend Seymour before he departed.

"I covet your prayers for a safe journey there and back, Preacher. Be safe. Who knows, maybe when I return, we can go on a spring hunt with bows and arrows: You, I, and Skiddy."

"I'll be practicing, Captain! God's grace be with you!" Seymour said with a smile.

CHAPTER EIGHT

Rachel Keyes Becomes Rachel Davis!

The voyage from Fort Saint George back to England was a long, tedious one with inclement weather and torrential storms, which included some illness entering into the new year, but at least there were no deaths to report.

1607 had been a year of much planning and effort by the London Company with its Plymouth and Virginia Charters: the Plymouth Charter and its founding of the Popham Colony, and the Virginia Charter with its founding of the Jamestown Colony. The start of such endeavors were filled with much excitement. So much attention and accolades were given those who were in the leadership roles, of which the Davis family was prevalent. James knew how the Popham Colony had faired but was looking forward to hearing how the Jamestown Colony was doing in comparison.

In reflecting over the year, James Davis had mixed emotions. He too, had experienced the excitement of the new adventure and enjoyed the limelight he received by the English aristocrats. He was proud to be representing the Crown; what an honor it was. He also felt fulfilled in being able to travel with his older brother Robert, of whom he finally got to see all of the skills he possessed first hand. The stories he grew up with were indeed true.

Perhaps the most significant emotion of the year came undeniably at the meeting of Rachel Keyes. James made the decision that when he saw her again, he would ask for her hand in marriage. He couldn't help but wonder if his quick decision to be the one to navigate the *Gift* was somewhat moved by his desire to see her again. "After all," he questioned to himself, "How can you pray for someone and write them every night without growing close to them?"

The *Gift of God* arrived in Plymouth Harbor on February 27, 1608. James was relieved to see the *Mary and*

John anchored at the dock upon arriving in the harbor. Now at least he knew his brother Robert made it home safely, but was confused that there was no obvious activity upon the ship. It should have been preparing for the supply trip back to the Popham Colony. Having sailed a mere two months after she left the colony, the *Gift* finally was finally anchored alongside the *Mary and John* again.

James quickly gathered his belongings and boarded the carriage to take him to the Davis estate. It was a great, unexpected reunion when he arrived. Every one of his brothers were home, including his brother Robert. After all of the welcoming was over, James met with both his father and his brother in his father's study.

"I have to say I'm surprised to see you still here, Robert," James remarked with somewhat of an attitude. "Did you forget there is an entire settlement waiting for supplies? What has kept you from returning?"

Robert was surprised by James' assuming he didn't care about the colony when he realized he was unaware of the circumstances. "Hold on, little brother. All I have been doing since I returned has been working to get the aid needed for the colony! Were you aware Sir John Popham had died?"

James was dumbfounded, "No. When did that happen?"

"Just ten days after we originally departed last May. It was unexpected but when I was getting ready to bring the letter from President Popham to his uncle, Father told me the news. He also informed me of the low moral of the investors as a result. We've been meeting with the investors individually to convince them that the colony is worth their money. Actually, Rachel Keyes has been a large influence in that arena! She believes in you and what you are doing! But now, you came home with half the colony? What image does that portray?" inquired Robert.

James was upset over the turn of events but now understood the delay Robert was experiencing. He also remembered the letter given to him by the President.

"I have a letter from President Popham here to give to

his uncle." He pulled out the letter. "He wrote it in Latin, knowing no one but his uncle would be able to translate it if it fell into the wrong hands. He wanted to make sure this was communicated to the investors."

"I can read it," their father said, "Hand it to me. Let me read what it says."

Thomas took the letter and slowly read it but looked a little confused. The two sons could tell there was something wrong. "What is it, Father?"

"This letter doesn't line up with what you have communicated to me thus far, but I'm sure it would get investors excited. He says that everything has gone better than anticipated. Fort St. George is complete and fully operational. The Indians have been very trusting and giving them huge stashes of traded fur and showed them where they could find rocks full of precious metals. He said there is tobacco galore and he's even got wind from more than a few sources of natives that there is a large water passage-way to the southern ocean just seven days away, just as we suspected."

Robert and James looked at each other and laughed. "He is definitely fearful of not keeping the investors optimistic. He probably suspected something when Robert didn't return right away with supplies. It's amazing how your mind will play tricks on you when you are trying to stay warm surrounded by ice," explained James.

"The president might have embellished the report a bit," explained Robert, "but the truth of the matter, Father, is that with the needed supplies, winter being over, and now with those gone who didn't have the fortitude to stick it out, the Popham Colony has a great chance to succeed! It is truly a beautiful land with lots of forests for acquiring lumber for construction."

James looked at Robert and asked, "You said Rachel was helping you turn the minds of the investors? How is she doing that? You sound as if you see her often."

Robert responded, "Any chance she gets to be around our family, she takes it. She has won all of our hearts, brother! We have an appointment with Sir Radcliff tomorrow, so she will be here in the morning. I can't wait to see the look on her face when she sees you."

Their servant, Joseph, came into the room. "Dinner is ready, Sirs."

"Who's up for some food?" asked Thomas, "When was the last time you ate food prepared by someone other than a ship's cook, James? We have set quite a table for you, my adventurous son!" The Davis family enjoyed the remainder of the day, sharing stories of their adventures.

All evening long, James rehearsed what the moment will be like when he and Rachel see each other again. He grew more nervous as he imagined how he would ask her to marry him. Should he get down on one knee with his hat pulled to his chest and ask her? No, that would be too formal and Rachel is more fun than formal. Should he sit next to her on the swing, look into her eyes and with his own eyebrow lifted in a casual, but somehow gallant way, form the words, "Rachel, will you be my wife?" That just doesn't seem right.

He continued to imagine different ways he should ask until finally he devised what he felt would be a most creative plan.

The morning arrived and finally after breakfast the coach containing Rachel Keyes came through the gate to the Davis estate. James watched as the coachman assisted his red-haired beauty to the walkway. As she looked up, she saw James on the porch with a huge smile on his bearded face. She dropped her bag and ran towards him, her hat falling to the ground, and the two met half way down the walk with James swinging her around in a loving embrace.

"James! I've missed you so much!" she said as she kissed him.

"And I, you Rachel!" They sat on the bench by the porch.

"Are you home for good James? Your brother and I have been busy acquiring the funds for supplies to send back to you at the colony. So, there's no need for that any longer?" Rachel asked.

"No, I wish I could say I am here for good but I'm

just here to help get the supplies as well. I'll fill you in on all that has happened but right now, let's enjoy this moment. Robert can go to the appointment with Sir Radcliff by himself. You and I can spend some time together. Want to walk in the garden, Rachel?" James asked.

The two walked arm in arm into the garden and stopped in front of a Glastonbury Hawthorn plant.

"I'll never forget the night we first met. Our first conversation was about all the magical stories of this *fairy* plant here." He pointed to the plant in front of them. "Then you said something that has haunted me ever since: Whether any of those legends are true, I don't know, but stories, legends, and tales make our imaginations soar, our lives fun and interesting!"

James reached into his sack and pulled out the journal and handed it to Rachel. "Here's my book, *A Relation of a Voyage to Sagadahoc.* It's full of stories, tales, and what will someday be legends. As I promised, I made daily accounts of my journey so we could share them together. I also prayed every night for you Rachel, as I entered the day's events. Why don't you open it up and I'll give you a glimpse of how it is."

Rachel looked loving in his eyes as she turned to the first page of the journal and read aloud, "Departed from the Lizard the first day of June 1607, being Monday about six o'clock in the afternoon and sailed northeast by north for eight leagues. From thence, I directed our course for the Islands of Flores and Corvo."

Rachel stopped and looked again at James. "Oh, this is going to be so interesting to read, James. I'm so impressed…What a lot of work you have done!"

"Look at the next page, Rachel." James directed her to open to the next page where she found an envelope with an outline of a heart, filled with intricate sketches of wildflowers, drawn on the front of it.

"What is this, James?"

"Whenever I thought of you, dear Rachel, I remembered watching you clip and arrange the beautiful flowers in your garden. That memory filled my heart, as this illustration shows. Open it up Rachel and see what it says." James placed his head next to hers and lightly rested it on her shoulder as she opened the envelope up to find a parchment with the following note written with red ink: *A Relation of the Voyage to Becoming Rachel Davis.*

Tears formed in Rachel's eyes as she looked over her shoulder at James.

"Rachel, will you be my wife?"

"Yes, James, Yes!" They kissed. "But you'll have to promise me, we'll live a life full of fun; and legendary adventures!"

The two of them went in the house to share the good news of their engagement to the Davis family.

Over the next few weeks, plans for the wedding were made. Both the Davis and Keyes families were pushing for a large, ceremonial wedding in the Exeter Cathedral by the Bishop himself, but Rachel desired a much smaller, simpler one at her home parish church of St. Thomas. So plans were made with the Vicar there.

The Keyes family held onto the old Celtic tradition of *"Handfasting."* Every marriage in the Keyes family partook of this ceremony when marriage vows were made. Rachel and her family would have it no other way. In this ceremony, couples literally bound their hands together with rope or cloth. It symbolized their strong love for each other and ended with them tying a fisherman's knot out of the cord that was binding their hands together. The finished knot when the ends were pulled, was so strong that the rope itself would break before the knot did. As the old tradition modernized, people had begun rather loosely giving the ceremony names like *"tying the knot,"* giving your *"hand in marriage"* or pronouncing the *"bonds of matrimony."*

The wedding was a beautiful church wedding with Rachel's favorite flowers decorating the aisle and entwined within the vale of her gown. After the vows were made and communion was received, the ropes were intertwined on their hands and the Vicar instructed James and Rachel, "Please tie the knot and pull the ends of your rope."

The bride and groom did and then the Vicar finished with, "May this knot be a reminder of the strength of your love and the binding of your hearts together! I announce to the congregation, Sir James and Lady Rachel Davis!"

At that final announcement, the crowd applauded as the couple departed to the carriage and drove off in the distance.

CHAPTER NINE

The Gift of God Returns

The time came for James to depart on the *Gift of God* with the fresh supplies back to the Popham Colony. He and Rachel had only been married for a week at the time but they both knew it was inevitable. Because so many of the colonists left with James back in December, the urgency was lightened some, but those left behind were anxiously waiting for new goods to arrive. They were unaware of all of the things that had happened since the departure of Captain Robert and the *Mary and John*. They knew nothing of the death of Sir John Popham, or of the resulting disillusion of the investors.

Once the winter was over and the snow began to melt, Master Digby the shipwright and his crew began working again on the *Virginia*. Digby had a stellar reputation as a shipwright in London and had been specifically selected by the Virginia Company to construct a ship, or pinnace, at the new settlement that would be strong and stout enough to carry heavy cargos of furs, metals, and fish, yet small enough to travel up the rivers nearby as well as the ocean.

Master Digby estimated the ship would need to be about fifty feet long, sixteen feet wide, and draw about six feet deep into the water. It would have a carrying capacity of roughly 30 tons. It was known that he would be using whatever resources were available at the colony but some additional resources, such as sail cloth, rope, and two four-hundred pound anchors forged from iron, had been already been included in the cargo of the *Mary and John* when it first departed.

Wood was plentiful for the boat, so that was no issue. Planks were being finished for the decks from the abundance of pine logs. The ship's carpenters first found a stout oak, from which they were able to hewn out the perfect forty-foot starter log. It took ten of them three full days just to cut it and successfully manhandle it into place at the deep construction dam prepared next to the fort. Due to the rocky soil, digging the pit alone was a larger project than expected.

James bid farewell to his new bride. Rachel came to see him off at the *Gift* and the two were outside of his cabin making future plans.

"Of course I understand your commission as Captain and I married you with the knowledge that your love would always be split between two passions: your family and the sea. But that doesn't keep me from confessing I wish I were going with you, James."

James responded, "I've thought long on the subject, Rachel, and once I'm confident the colony is safe and success is guaranteed, then you can join me and we can start our family in the new world. People talk about how adventurous we seamen are but I've never been around a more adventurous woman than you, Love. I'll come back for you soon!"

"There's nothing that would please me more, James!

Go in peace and know you will be in my prayers." With the last goodbye being said, James and Rachel kissed one last time before she left the ship. She watched proudly as the rigging was released and the *Gift of God* set sail out of Plymouth Harbor.

Now, James focused on the task at hand. Get the supplies to Fort St. George as quickly as possible while the weather is permitting and the days are long. Day after day, they navigated along the same route followed a few months earlier. When they passed St. George Island, the one with the cross, he couldn't help but reflect back to the sermon delivered by Reverend Seymour. He looked forward to seeing his friend again and seeing the progress made on the colony while he was away.

The *Gift of God* arrived at Fort St. George in May 1608. The fort was a welcomed site. James hadn't seen the fort and its tall, angled stone walls, complete with cannons from this vantage point before. It was quite impressive; much different in the warm, early-summer sunlight than the snowy,

December morning when he departed. The crew began unloading supplies while James went ashore, meeting the preacher at the beach.

"Wonderful to see you again, Captain!" Seymour exclaimed as they shook hands.

"How is everyone faring, Richard?" looking around at the foreboding walls and entrance gate, "Oh my, how things have improved here! I'd like to speak to President Popham. Can you take me to him?"

"Captain, things have indeed changed around here. First off, Sir Popham has died," said Seymour, "The winter weather just kept getting worse after you left. Our firewood supply was dwindling quickly and the new wood was too green to burn. The clay houses we made were just no match for the cold weather. Popham wasn't in the best of health as it was. He was complaining much about his joints, and all. He got to where he refused to leave his abode and stayed in his bed until one morning back in February, I went to bring him some food and discovered him lifeless in his bed. It is indeed a miracle that more lives weren't lost, James!"

James wasn't expecting to hear such a report. "So, is Admiral Gilbert in charge now?" asked James.

"Yes, Captain. Actually, the Admiral has been commanding the fort ever since you left. As Popham grew weaker, the men looked to Gilbert as their leader. He's not here right now. He took the shallop and a group of men to explore up the coast a bit, still trying to make amends with the natives. You know the Admiral, he's not one to stay put where there is no adventure. Therefore much of the Admiral's time is spent exploring. In the meanwhile, the carpenters, shipwrights, blacksmith and cooper have continued to finish their projects here at the fort. Walk with me James, let me show you the latest!"

The two men walked through the gate into the fort, looking at the new Gentlemen houses, the officer's dwellings, the storehouse, kitchen, and the chapel, now complete with a carved crucifix above the altar.

"One last thing to show you, Captain!" said Richard.

They walked around to the other side of the fort, where construction on the *Virginia* had begun just before James left in December. Now, he could see a beautiful pinnace, still in dry dock, but a determined crew of carpenters at work. James and the preacher met up with Master Digby the shipwright. He was proud of the ship and those who had been relentlessly working on it.

"The English can say anything they wish about how we weren't able to farm the land but one thing's for sure," Digby boasted, "we definitely know how to build a ship! I've built ships in London all my life, have a stellar reputation, and this beauty is one to rival the best I've seen, Captain!"

"It is a beauty! When will we be able to launch?"

"Provided all goes as it has been, we should be able to launch in just a few days!" responded Master Digby.

While they were touring the fort, the boats returned with Admiral Gilbert and his men. One boat was packed full of furs, sassafras, and cinnamon. Gilbert met James in the center of the fort. The planters, carpenters and crew were all assembled, welcoming Captain James back to the colony, so he decided to take this opportunity to address them publically.

"Men, I have to say I am impressed by all you have achieved in my absence. I'm sorry to hear about the fate of dear, President Popham, but I have some news I need to bring to you as well. I know you have wondered why there was such a delay in bringing supplies to you, so I need to give you an explanation."

"When my brother, Captain Robert Davis, arrived in Plymouth, he found that the leader of our charter, Sir John Popham, had died just ten days after we left England. As a result, the support for the colony was deteriorating and Captain Robert had the job of reestablishing the financial support of the investors. We now have full support again."

The crowd cheered for the news.

"Any news of how our rival, the Colony in Jamestown, is doing Captain?" asked one of the men.

"All I've heard was that they, like us, faced a brutal

winter as well. We only had one casualty, and they had many. Their supply mission was departing the harbor at the same time as ours. So, keep them in your prayers. No one can understand what they've gone through better than we can," answered James.

The men were overjoyed to have James back commanding the fort. Leadership had taken many different roads during the past 9 months. They had gone from the military leadership of Captain James to a style that resembled a parental-type leadership of President Popham, and then to a leader who desires to make a name for himself as an explorer. The colonists felt pretty much on their own. James became somewhat of a hero in their eyes, now that he brought back supplies and put the colony first place. He and Admiral Gilbert stepped aside to talk.

"From the looks of things, Admiral, I'm assuming trade with the natives is going well. Still in contact with Skidwarres?"

Gilbert responded, "Skidwarres and Dehenada

haven't been around for a while now. They led us up river to a tribe and helped us establish favorable relations with them. We've been trading with them since, but it is a rather volatile connection. It appears the chief of their tribe has a vendetta to pay to a neighboring tribe whose chief killed his son in a skirmish between the two tribes. He has welcomed us with open arms because the English represent power and force. We have attempted to establish trade with the other tribe but there is always opposition. When I heard the *Gift* had arrived, I came here straightway but left a few men there to finish transactions. Roger Higgins is in charge of them."

Suddenly, an arrow appeared from over the wall of the fort, barely missing the Admiral and lodging into the post near where he was standing. The howling cry of the natives could be heard getting louder as they neared the fort. A few more arrows came over the wall. Digby, and the carpenters working on the *Virginia* came running into the fort. There was the sound of a musket being discharged. Then another musket fired.

Roger Higgins and his men came running through the gate carrying their firearms, seeking refuge, and the gate to the fort was closed behind them. Higgins had been hit in the arm with an arrow and was bleeding. The men took their places on the walls. The sound of the war cry outside was deafening.

At Captain James' command, the crew loaded the wall cannon. Once given the nod, they lit the fuse and the cannon fired into the forest with such a loud, piercing blast that everyone was startled. A large pine tree was hit and fell as a result, nearly hitting the natives standing at its base. They ran back into the forest in terror.

Higgins and his men were sitting, leaning against the gate. He was holding a rag to his wound.

"Well, now we know how the chief reacts to one of us getting fresh with his daughter!" Higgins commented to one of his men. The men laughed at his comment.

"She was sure a looker!" said one man.

"Aye, you shouldn't have tried to kiss her though,

Higgins! You almost got us all killed!" replied another.

Captain James overheard the men and their conversation. He walked over to Roger Higgins and told him to stand. He did. Then James threw a punch that landed in his face! "You idiot! You put this entire colony at risk and laugh about it as well?" He motioned for Marshall Ellis to come over. "Throw him in the brig and see to it that the physician sees his arm."

James walked back over to Gilbert who was shaking his head in unbelief.

"Well, so much for that connection, Admiral."

"Let's face it, Captain, it isn't wise to only have men as planters of a colony, and as we have seen, it isn't safe either. There needs to be women colonists as well. The men are needy of their attention. Men will be men after all." Then, he looked directly at Captain James, "To be honest, I'm quite bored. Today was a rather exhilarating change of pace. I'm happy you are back to take charge of the fort. It's one less mundane, domestic burden on me. Now I can focus once again on charting the costal area of the Sagadahoc, establishing trade and doing what I do best."

James thought to himself, "With such leadership, I am amazed there is still a colony present."

Fort St George remained closed and guarded for the remainder of the day to make sure all danger was gone. The next morning, the fort's gate opened and it was business as usual. Everyone continued their tasks from the day before.

After about a week, Master Digby came to Captain James with the good news. The *Virginia* was ready to be launched! Digby got word to all in the fort and they assembled next to the pit where construction had been taking place. Rev. Seymour came wearing his vestment and Bible in hand as James addressed the crowd.

"Today, we are making history once again for England and the Crown!" James exclaimed, "Until this point in time, there has not been a ship constructed and launched in the Americas. It is appropriate that we name her the *Virginia* after all, since she was built here in what is called Virginia

Territory. Mastor Digby deserves an applause for seeing this project through in spite of all the obstacles encountered."

Master Digby took off his cap and raised his arms in a worshipful gesture towards the sky while all clapped. Reverend Seymour approached the head of the crowd and addressed them.

"Let us pray, christening and commissioning this vessel to the work of the Lord and the King. Please bow your heads." Everyone removed their caps in reverence and bowed their heads.

"Almighty God. Today we dedicate this vessel, the *Virginia*, to you. In Psalm 91, you tell us that you will give your angels charge over us and keep us in all of our ways. We ask for your angelic protection over this ship and those commanding it."

When Seymour was finished, Captain James nodded to the men on shore at the bow of the vessel where they broke open the dam allowing the water to rush in and quickly fill the construction pit. The *Virginia* could now float for the first time.

The excitement was great, and for the first time in months, the carpenters and builders were able to spend a day of fun as a reward to all of their hard work and diligence. There was a celebration in the Courtyard full of music, beer, wine, and fish galore!

There were sixty planters and crew left at the colony. A small group compared to the first who came last year, but still able to accomplish great things under some strong leadership. Most of the farmers had left with James at the onset of the previous winter, but there were still a few who decided to till the soil near the fort to plant vegetables for a first crop, to prohibit another famine and prepare for the upcoming seasons.

Admiral Gilbert wasted no time organizing an expedition with twenty of the men using the new *Virginia* as their vessel to travel farther south with the hopes of discovering some precious ore, spices, and establishing trade with the different native tribes.

The Virginia Company had established the two ventures: The Plymouth Company which included the Popham Settlement, and the London Company which included the Jamestown Settlement 850 miles to the south. The costal area between the two settlements, and one hundred miles inland, was declared by King James as open territory for exploration and settlement with approval. It was this area that provided the most opportunity for resources, and now with the *Virginia* at their disposal, they had a vessel capable of safely making longer trips.

The tension between the local natives and the fort continued to escalate. Occasionally, some of the tools and fort supplies showed up missing. The natives were suspected as the thieves. It appeared they would do whatever they could to cause the settlement to fail.

The farmers were successful at growing beans, squash, and fields of corn as well. As harvest time arrived however, a fire occurred in the cornfield causing the farmers to have labored in vain. There was never any proof, but those at the fort were convinced the natives started the fire. All of this contributed to a new low morale of the men.

Captain James called a meeting with Reverend Seymour, Admiral Gilbert, and Marshal Ellis to address the issue.

"In order for the colony to succeed, gentlemen, we need to reestablish a positive relation with the local natives," stated James. "We cannot continue always looking over our shoulders, trying to anticipate their next move."

Admiral Gilbert threw up his arms in amazement, "We don't need those varmints! I'm getting enough trade with the tribes down the coast. If we show them our strength, they'll leave us alone."

Reverend Seymour added, "I agree with Captain James. We'll only be able to prosper as a colony if we are at peace with our neighbors."

"You say that because you've been taken in by them, preacher! After all, your best friend is none other than Skidwarres! Can't you see that as Englishmen, we are superior?" retorted Gilbert.

"I must disagree with you, Admiral," said James, "We're are either going to focus on building the colony our investors want, or we are going to focus on exploring the new world. We can't do both, but we seem to be trying to! The men are divided as well."

Admiral Gilbert was obviously not in agreement with what James and the Reverend concluded. "How about you, Marshal Ellis? I'm curious to hear what you have to say."

"I have the privilege to break up the quarrels and fights among the men," Ellis responded sarcastically, "When Popham died and you became leader, Admiral, you had full support of the men. Now that Captain James has returned and assumed leadership of the fort, the men don't know whom to follow. Two strong leaders, you Admiral, and you Captain. We need to make a decision. What is our focus as a colony? Why are we here? The answer in my opinion is to establish a prosperous settlement for the King and our investors. I have to agree with making peace. I urge you Admiral, to focus on building a prosperous colony."

The Admiral was reluctant to put the quest for adventure aside so the colony itself could be strongly established. "So, there's only one solution to the division that has arisen. A challenge between you and I, Captain James! If I win, the men follow me, if you win they follow you."

Raleigh Gilbert stood up and knocked over his chair in disgust, drawing attention to himself and shouted, "Captain James, I hereby challenge you to a duel of fisticuffs! Anything with two heads is a freak of nature and there is only room for one commander of this colony! Are you man enough to accept the challenge?"

The men around them were at full attention now. Looking to see how their captain was going to react. Men, especially soldiers, are always up for a good fight. Those who were fed up with Gilbert's followers cheered James on.

"Man enough? Ha!" James retorted, "You make me laugh, Gilbert! You and your fancy clothes and long, curly hair ask me if I'm *MAN* enough? If you want a challenge of fisticuffs, I'll give you one you'll most surely regret!"

Both men held up their fists while the onlookers cheered. Marshal Ellis, the peace-keeper, interjected some rules, "We will go outside, Gentlemen, into the courtyard."

The crowd followed and Ellis assigned two men to wrap the hands of James and Gilbert with strips of leather so no bones would be broken. Captain James removed his cap and his jacket and stood on one side of center of the courtyard while Admiral Gilbert stood on the other side, facing his opponent. Both men were equally qualified and trained to protect themselves.

The Marshal blew his whistle to start the bout. The two men came together face-to-face and circled one another amongst the cheering crowd with their fists in the air. They were obviously evaluating the tactics to use when James threw the first punch, a jab at Gilbert's chest, blocked by Gilbert's arms.

Gilbert in turn threw an overhand punch coming downward on James' shoulder. At this time, James threw a hook and hit Gilbert in the face, knocking off the admiral's long-haired wig, exposing his balding head. The onlookers laughed.

The two men continued to throw punches, and by now, both of their noses were bleeding. Gilbert used a move he learned in Academy that was called "Playing Possum," which is where he pretended to be hurt so that James would attack aggressively but with his guard down so he was vulnerable. It worked and Gilbert was able to throw a couple of very effective jabs into James' midsection, briefly knocking the wind out of him.

At this time, Gilbert thought he had the victory as James appeared to have faded, which is a term used meaning "run out of energy." As he aggressively went in to finish James off, James hit him with an uppercut punch to the chin followed by another jab to his face. To James' surprise, that last jab was all it took to see Gilbert's eyes move up into his brow and him fall face-down onto the dirt!

James stood looking at Gilbert on the ground

unconscious while the men, cheering and shouting for him, held up his arm in victory!

"James Davis! James Davis! James Davis!" the men repeatedly shouted as two men came under his legs, lifted him up and carried him around the courtyard in celebratory display.

The decision had been settled once and for all. The true Commander of Fort St. George was Captain James Davis.

CHAPTER TEN

Raleigh Gilbert's Surprise

"Ship on the Horizon!" shouted the sentry on the east wall of Fort St. George. This proclamation stirred all in the fort, wondering who could be sailing so near. All hands took their places on the walls to man the cannons if needed. Looking through the spyglass, the sentry followed it up with, "It's the *Mary and John*! The *Mary and John*, I say!"

It was September 10, 1608 and the ship anchored next to the *Gift of God*. Captained by Robert Davis, the boat was bringing fresh supplies for the Popham Colony. Captain James was on the shore to greet his brother Robert as the longboat arrived.

Robert looked around at the tall walls of the fort in amazement and then saw the completed pinnace, *Virginia* in the small bay to the side. They had accomplished so much within the past eleven months! James was thrilled to see his brother's bearded smile once again.

"What is the state of the colony, little Brother?" asked Robert as they hugged each other. Robert lifted a large canvas bag from inside of the longboat. Inside were letters and other correspondence from England. "Greetings from Father, Mother, and of course Rachel sends her love, along with this letter." Robert handed James an envelope.

"We are still making a go of it, Robert. It has been hard work but the few men I have here are determined to make the venture successful for our investors in England," said James.

He opened the letter from Rachel, read it quickly, and with a big smile, folded it and placed it in his pocket to enjoy later. He turned to Marshall Ellis and told him, "Please pass the word to the men that my brother Robert has brought letters for them." Ellis took the bag and placed it in the center of the fort, outside of the chapel.

James filled Robert in on the events that happened at

the fort since his return and the two enjoyed a meal together before Admiral Gilbert joined them with news they did not expect.

"I received letters from my family and their attorney," said Gilbert, "It appears my older brother John has taken ill and died. He and his wife were childless, so I am inheriting a great portion of the Gilbert Manor in Devon. I must return in order to make it legal."

"First, I must say I am sorry for your loss, Gilbert," commented James, "Second, I must say that if you depart back to England, these men who have an allegiance to you will want to follow suit. Is there anything we can do to convince you to stay? For the sake of the colony?"

"My dear friends look around at these makeshift cottages, the dirt floors within, and tell me how they compare to the wonderful grounds of Gilbert Manor. The prestige of ownership to those in authority around Devon far outweighs the alliance of these few men in this God-forsaken outpost. I'm making plans to leave and inherit what is rightfully mine," he said with arrogance.

Word traveled quickly around the fort. Admiral Gilbert was planning on leaving and was very vocal about it with his comrades. As Captain James said, it wasn't long before those who were aligned with Gilbert talked about leaving as well.

"We aren't farmers. We aren't carpenters. With the Admiral leaving, what is our purpose for staying? We have very little in common with those who wish to stay," they grumbled.

Captains James and Robert called a meeting with all those at the settlement to make one last attempt to convince them not to abandon the Popham Colony. They needed to determine how many had intentions on leaving and how many were staying. In doing so, they would determine whether they should continue to even have the settlement.

"Gentlemen, I want to remind you of all you've accomplished here at Fort St. George! Look out over the settlement. Please take a moment to do so," James paused for a moment to emphasize that point.

"There is much that you can consider dear to your hearts. You've constructed a fort greater than most back in England: those walls, those cottages, cooperage and chapel. You finally have some crops being harvested. Lastly, look at that beautiful little ship you've constructed! All of these accomplishments will only be in your memories should we have to uproot and move back to England because of a lack of support here."

"So my question for you fine gentlemen is," James continued, "How many of you are willing to stick it out here in the Popham Colony and how many of you wish to go home? If there is not enough to man the settlement and the fort, then we shall all return to England."

James again paused for a moment to let the reality set in for the future of the Popham Colony, then he concluded with, "The time has come, brothers. Please raise your hand if you desire to stay at the fort." He and his brother Robert raised their hands to encourage the others. Then they counted the raised hands.

There were a total of 14 hands raised, including theirs. The remaining 45 colonists had decided to return to England.

The reality that the colony was coming to a close was finally settling in and plans were needed for departure. With the death of their President and now Admiral Gilbert's decision to move home, there was no convincing them to stay.

"James, I need to tell you about a concern I have," Robert said, "Fort St. George is now a fully-operable military outpost. I'm concerned that if we leave the fort unoccupied, it won't be long before someone occupies it…perhaps even someone we don't want to. What would keep the Spanish from turning it into an outpost for Spain? All of the hard work we English put into this fort, only to have it go into our rival's possession?"

James understood the concern his brother had. "I see what you are saying, Brother, that would be absolutely the worst. To think that the Spaniards aren't aware of Ft. St George is ridiculous. Everyone knows about the Virginia Company's charters."

"Remember how the Dutch told us there were Spanish spies everywhere?" Robert stated, "I think I my ship's master, Anthony, was our spy! When I first returned to Plymouth for supplies, Anthony stole the layout of Fort St. George I was taking to Sir John Popham right off my desk. I couldn't locate him after that. If that drawing got into Spanish hands, they know every detail about the Fort!"

"As much as I don't want to do it, we must destroy the fort before we leave. After we remove everything we can, we will have to set it on fire and destroy anything that can be used by someone else! Are you in agreement, Robert?"

Robert nodded his head in agreement and the two began to make plans for the destruction of the fort they worked so hard to build.

Captain James divided the men into teams and over the next week, systematically went from cottage to cottage, each gentleman's home and other buildings packing up anything worth keeping. Rev. Seymour requested specifically for the newly carved cross at the chapel's altar to be placed in his care for the trip back to England.

It was decided that James Davis would be Captain of the *Virginia* and would carry the majority of the planters on board with him. Robert Davis would be Captain of the *Mary and John* and Raleigh Gilbert would be Captain of the *Gift of God*.

It was a tedious job to load the cannons and all of the remaining valuables onto the ships, but at last, they were ready to depart. Captain James, his brother Robert, and Reverend Seymour walked one last time through the abandoned fort. They stood in front of the remaining walls of the fort's chapel.

"Can I get you to pray one last time in your chapel, Preacher?" James asked, "I feel God blessed us with this settlement from the beginning, but now we're giving it back to Him. I'm thankful for the times we had here, as short as it was, and for the friends made. We are also leaving the body of one of our dear friends, Sir George Popham in the land he wanted to claim as his own. God has watched over us all so far, but now we will need His blessing on our trip home as well."

Rev. Seymour took charge at this time. "Please kneel with me, men. Our merciful God and Father, we thank you for all you have done for us at this colony. I thank you for those who have converted their lives to you while we were here. I thank you for the many miracles that we saw and lives saved during difficult times. Now, as we close this chapter in our lives with you, we ask for your protection and guidance as we travel back home to England. May our way be filled with peace and may the weather be in our favor as well. We pray this in the name of the Father, the Son, and the Holy Spirit, Amen."

The men added their "Amen" also, but suddenly there was a loud "Amen!" from the edge of the wall. All were startled by the shout and turned to see none other than their old friend, Skidwarres.

"Skiddy!" shouted the preacher, "I didn't think I would ever see you again!" He ran and tenderly gave his old pupil a large hug. "I'm going to miss you, Skiddy!"

"Me too will miss you, my brother in the Lord. I got word you departing and me wanted to say farewell. Thank you Preacher for teaching me English, for saving my life, for teaching me Christian faith and bringing me home to my family." Skidwarres said in his broken English

"I brought you and Captain James a gift to remember Skidwarres." Skidwarres pulled out two fine bows from his bag and handed them to the men. "This so you remember *you* not only one to teach, Preacher. Skidwarres teach *you* something too! And you, Captain, you need practice your skills too!"

"I gladly accept your gift," replied James. The two shook hands as they bid him farewell for the last time. Skidwarres met up with his family and departed into the forest.

Captain Robert fashioned an explosive mound with the gunpowder in the now-abandoned storehouse. They also set some dry logs and boards around the buildings realizing the only way to totally demolish the fort is by fire. The three men set the logs on fire and watched the walls go up in flames as they boarded the longboat for their boats anchored off shore.

The ships hoisted anchors and set sail with the smoke from the colony on the shore behind them. Suddenly, the gunpowder exploded and the walls tumbled down, securing that no one again would ever use the fort as a stronghold.

This was official the end of what was known as the Popham Colony! From this point, the focus would have to be to bring everyone home safely. As for James, he was mixed with regret for the colony and excitement for seeing his wife Rachel again.

He departed Plymouth with the hopes of strengthening the colony and then coming home to get his wife so they could move there and establish a home together in the new world. Now, that looked as if it would never happen. He began trying to plan where he and Rachel would live to establish their new family. For both of their personalities and motivations, moving to the Popham Colony was the answer but now that was no longer an option.

As James captained the *Virginia* to its new home, he admired the handiwork of the craftsmen who constructed it. Master Digby, the shipwright from London, and those commissioned to build the ship were now traveling on it as well, pointing out every personal feature, unique to the *Virginia*. James grew to appreciate the ship, It had been a while since he had been on such a new ship, let alone one of such high quality! As a result, the traveling time to Plymouth Harbor was much more enjoyable than before.

As they passed the Lizard Lighthouse, Captain James was reminded of the many times he had passed by before and of the many different expeditions and purposes for sailing. The purpose to establish the Popham Colony was sure one expedition he would never forget. "I'm just 29 years old and have seen so much so far. I can't help but wonder what new adventures God has planned for me and my new wife Rachel to enjoy," James thought to himself.

The ships entered past the walls of the fort that just the year before had discharged cannons to celebrate the beginning of the expedition. They docked at the harbor, quickly gathered their belongings, and James and Robert departed towards the Davis Estate.

As they were leaving, they rode past a series of ships loading in the harbor. As they passed by the ship called the *Falcon*, Captain James asked the coachman where the ships were headed. "These ships are loading up for the next supply mission to the Jamestown Colony in Virginia," the coachman explained.

They had to travel slowly down the dock due to all of the foot traffic. Suddenly, James spotted a familiar face in the crowd. It was Captain John Martin. John's father, Sir Richard Martin was a good friend of James' father, Thomas. He had been the Lord Mayor of London and a frequent visitor of the Davis Estate while James was a child. James asked the coachman to stop and waved for Captain Martin to stop. Martin was surprised and delighted to see James and Robert.

"John ol' boy! How goes it?" asked James, "Are you part of the supply mission to Jamestown? Have you been yet?"

"Aye, James, I have! I've been part of the Virginia Company's London Charter since it's conception." He thought for a moment. "You are a part of the Virginia Company's Plymouth Charter! What are you doing home? Last I heard, you established the Popham Colony and you were the Captain at Fort St George."

"Things didn't go as planned, John. We no sooner left than Sir John Popham died. Then we had a rough winter and many of the planters came home. Then President George Popham died, leaving Sir Raleigh Gilbert in charge while I was gone. But then, Gilbert got word that his brother died and he is inheriting much property, so he came back and the colony is now officially over."

"Did you enjoy the new territory?" asked John, "It has gotten into *my* bones!"

"That's one way to put it, John," said James, "I guess you could say it has *gotten into my bones* as well! I didn't want to leave. Why do you ask?"

"I ask because we are looking for some more planters in Virginia. We're bringing back a large group of farmers, carpenters and masons to expand the colony! I'm building a tobacco plantation of my own and the possibilities are outstanding! Right now, I need some men to commit to bring supplies back to Jamestown. I presently have my ship, the *Falcon*, Captain Webb's ship, the *Lion*, Captain Archer's ship, the *Blessing*, Captain Christopher's ship, the *Sea Adventure*, and Captain Wood's ship the *Unite*. I estimate I'm going to need four more ships to hold supplies and planters. Do you have a boat, James?"

"Actually, See that beautiful little Pinnace over there?" James smiled as he pointed to the *Virginia*. "That vessel is the first vessel ever built in the Americas, and I'm its Captain!"

"Why not join us, James?" John invited.

"I must say the offer is tempting to say the least, but I have a new wife now and I've been gone for six months already! I'm on my way to see her now!"

"Well, I understand James but please consider it. You can come to Virginia and build a plantation next to mine. I can even put a good word in for you with John Radcliff, Captain of Fort Algernon. He needs help and your experience at Fort St. George, would be a blessing!"

"Alright, Alright, John, I'll consider it but now I've got to go. Best wishes John!"

"Best wishes James!"

The captains each went their ways. As James and Robert rode along, James was focused on the road ahead. Robert asked James, "Why are you so quiet, Little Brother?" He paused for a moment, "Wait a minute, you're thinking about going with Captain Martin to Jamestown aren't you?"

Robert rolled his eyes, "James, you do have it *in your bones*, don't you?"

"Do me a favor, Little Brother," Robert said with his bearded smile, "Enjoy your wife for a few days before you spring the idea on her."

"Aye, Aye, Captain!" James smiled back at his brother as they rode along.

It wasn't long before they entered the gate of the Davis Estate. The family enjoyed each other's time together and after a week of enjoyment, Rachel finally asked James the inevitable question, "James, we need to decide what we are going to do. Where do you want to establish our own home? When do you want to begin a family of our own?"

This was the moment James was waiting for. He got a serious look on his face and then said, "Rachel, I love you. And I've been thinking about that for quite a while."

He brought his face three inches from hers, and holding her cheeks in the palm of his hands, he smiled and sincerely said, "Rachel, the third supply mission to the

Jamestown Colony is gathering supplies now and they are needing any available ships. I've decided to bring the *Virginia* full of supplies to Jamestown." As he spoke, he could see Rachel's disappointment start to display by tears forming in her eyes.

"But James, you just got back and now you are already planning on leaving again?" said Rachel, "How will we ever start a family if you're always gone?"

"No, Rachel. I want you to travel with me. We'll carry supplies there first, but we will stay and then you and I will build a home, a Tobacco Plantation of our own and start a family there in Jamestown!"

"Oh James! I love you! Jamestown, here we come!"

They kissed and a new adventure was about to begin.

THE END

THE STORY BEHIND THE STORY

As told by William Michael Bryan

This story is based upon historical fact but embellished with some artistic license. Captain James Davis was my 7th Great Grandfather on my mother's side. My mother was Eltra Ophelia Davis (1916-2001). It is based upon facts uncovered after having DNA testing done and the research that followed. There are many articles and historical accounts about the Popham Colony, the other participants of the voyage, Captain James Davis, his family and their contributions to the early founding of our country. I encourage you to check them out on your own.

The only written account of the voyage from England to the Popham Colony was the journal which James wrote along the way, *Relation of a Voyage to Sagadahoc*. It can be read in its original form on line. The manuscript remained hidden for 267 years. It was finally uncovered in 1875 when the late Rev. B.F. De Costa D.D was researching in the library of Lambeth Palace, London. He immediately made the manuscript public.

There was also a map or drawing of Fort St. George showing the exact layout of the fort that was presumed lost as well. However, now it is known that as a result of espionage, this map was sold to the Spanish Ambassador to London, Pedro de Zuniga, in 1608. The map was soon passed on to King Philip III of Spain. It remained hidden for 280 years until it was uncovered in the Spanish National Archives in 1888. I've included it at the end of this section.

Even though the venture of the Popham Colony ended as it did, the story of James and Rachel Davis continued to progress as follows: James and Rachel Davis joined the third supply mission to Jamestown traveling on the *Virginia*, thus immigrating to the Jamestown Colony, where James assumed command of Fort Algernon. Soon, James and Rachel built a plantation, settling outside of Jamestown and became leader of the fort at Henrico. They began their family there and all became leaders in the area. It is assumed that the Thomas Davis, who was a 1619 Burgess Representative in Jamestown, representing Captain Martin's district known as "Martin Brandon's Plantation," was James' father. He followed James to Henrico, where he became a leader. He is officially counted as "immigrated" with his wife Elizabeth when she arrived toward the end of 1619.

It is with great amazement that I can claim such a family of explorers and Early Colonists as my ancestors.

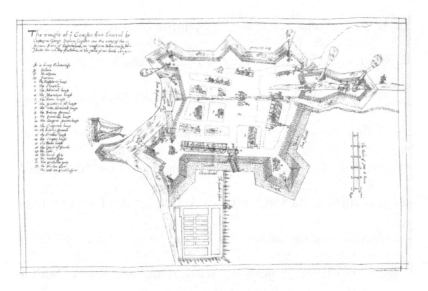

MAP OF FORT ST. GEORGE

Made in United States
Orlando, FL
20 July 2022

19987676R00114